THE PIANO OF DEATH

BOOKS BY CLARK

THE STAINS OF TIME

The Piano of Death

The Boot of Destiny

The Chains of Desire

The Elixir of Denial

The Dance of Dreams

OTHER BOOKS

Those Little Bastards

All He Left Behind

Missing Mr. Wingfield

The Seven Wives of Silver

Bad Poetry Night

Out of the Woods

Under the World

THE PIANO OF DEATH

E. CHRISTOPHER CLARK

Published in the United States by Clarkwoods in Chelmsford, Massachusetts.

ISBN for the Print Edition: 978-1-952044-10-6
ISBN for the Digital Edition: 978-1-952044-11-3

Library of Congress Control Number: 2020902235

For Stephanie, who came to see the very first play about Veronica on Valentine's Day 1998, then asked me out two days later

❧ I ❧
THE SNOWS OF
YESTERYEAR
DECEMBER 1999

I t began with a piano falling from the sky.

Veronica stepped onto the subway platform, guitar case in hand, and tried to shake the image from her mind. But just as the last whispers of the instrument's final cacophonous chord faded into a gentle hum, she caught sight of something that scared her even more.

It was a man, a *sales*man. He stood in his suit, leaning against a pillar, his nose in a book. It was Dickens, a collection if she'd read the spine correctly. But he didn't read, not him. She knew this man. He watched and he listened, but he did not read.

The Salesman looked up at her as she stepped tentatively toward him. He dog-eared the page he was on, then flashed her a wide smile. "Veronica," he said. "It's me. It's—"

"I don't know you," she said, turning away, stepping toward the yellow line that separated platform from track.

"You do," he said. "Or, well, you did. You did know me."

"Fine," said Veronica, listening as his footsteps grew closer. "I don't know you anymore."

"That can be fixed," he said, setting his hands upon her shoulders. "It can all be fixed."

She thought to shrug him off, so blatant was his bullshit. But he was selling her on it, the way he always did. How many times had the feel of his hands on her shoulders calmed her, comforted her? Whether it was on the swing set, each gentle push of his filling her with the bravery it took to swing higher and faster; or when she'd learned to ride her bike, and his lightest touch could right her most severe wobble; or at the piano, where even the suggestion of his hands nearby could convince her to power through the next measure.

The piano! She gestured toward the exit. "Did you see what happened out there?"

"I did," he said. "A shame. A real shame. Avoidable."

She turned on him, had to see in his eyes if he believed his own spin. "How?" she asked. "It was an accident. How do you avoid having a piano dropped on your head?"

"Stay away from high-priced high rises."

"Excuse me?" said Veronica.

"Stay away from places where a piano is likely to fall on you from an unsafe height and you are less likely to have a piano fall on your head." He smiled and ran his hands along her upper arms, giving her shoulders a squeeze as he said, "It's simple logic, sweetheart."

She stormed away from him, stared down the tunnel, squinting to see if she could make out any oncoming trains. "Don't call me that," she said. "You don't know me. You don't have the right."

"But I do," he said, his voice echoing through the empty station. "I've known you for longer than anyone else in the world, except perhaps your mother and the doctor who delivered you. Veronica," he said. "Look at me. It's me. It's—"

"Shut up," she said, frightened by the sound of her own voice, the authority it had as it bounced back at her. She looked around, disoriented. Where was everyone? Had the city shut this place down after the piano fell? But, if they had, why hadn't she and the

Salesman been evacuated, too? Something was going on here. "Where am I?" she said. "What is this place?"

"It's a subway platform," he said.

"Yes, I get that," she said, crossing to the map of the subway system, which showed not the Red and Green and Blue lines she was expecting, nor the Orange or the Silver, but instead a Purple line and a Yellow and a Black. She set a finger upon the Yellow Line and followed it to its terminus, a station named Oz. She shook her head. "I get that it's a subway platform," she said. "But is this real, or is it all happening inside my head?"

"Ah," he said. "Well, to quote one of your daughter's favorite books, 'Of course it is happening inside your head, but why on earth should that mean that it is not real?'"

She turned and faced him again. "Are you messing with me?" she asked.

He held a hand to his heart, trying to look affronted. "Would I ever?" he said.

"Yes," she said. "Yes, you would."

"I am not messing with you," said the Salesman.

Veronica tried to place the quote, but couldn't. And this surprised her. There were only so many books on their shelf at home, and she had read each of them to her daughter so many times. "What book is that from?" she said. "I don't recognize it."

"Of course not," he said. "It's what—when did you go to sleep? 1999?—That book hasn't even been published yet. But once you bring that one home, you're going to read it to her. Again and again."

Veronica scoffed. "You're from the future now, too?" She shook her head, paced. "It's that Chinese food that I ate that's causing this, isn't it? I have a friend who has this theory about crab rangoon being laced with marijuana. I never believed her, but—"

"Oh, be quiet Veronica, and I'll explain."

"Please do," she said.

He pulled his book out of his jacket pocket and began to thumb through it. "I can't remember the damned quotation," he said. "I nearly flunked out of school because of my English grades. I'm sure I told you that once."

She sighed, exasperated. "You never told us anything just once, Dad."

He smiled at the sound of the word, slapping his knee with the book as he did—slapping his knee! who still did that?—and then he let out a laugh. "You said it," he said. "You called me—"

"The quotation!" said Veronica. "Get on with it."

He returned to the book, put on his rough approximation of a British accent, and spoke: "I am here tonight to warn you that you have yet a chance and hope of escaping my fate."

She sighed. "*A Christmas Carol?*" she said. "So, who are you supposed to be? Marley? My father's not dead yet."

He slipped the book back into his jacket pocket. "Allow me some artistic license, if you please."

"As if I have a choice," she said.

"I am all of the ghosts in one," he said. "So many of you have asked, over the years, to have all of us at once, that we figured we might as well acquiesce."

"That's kind of you," she said, stepping again toward the edge of the platform, looking in both directions for a train out of there. "Now, can we get on with it?" she asked. "I'd like to get some actual rest before Tracy wakes up to bitch at me about the latest wrongs I've done her."

The Salesman slipped up beside her and asked, in almost a whisper, "Do you regret having her, Veronica? Do you often wonder what life would be like if—"

"Hey," she said. "Wait. Is this *A Christmas Carol* or *It's a Wonderful Life* that I'm dreaming here? It's not some mashup, is it?"

He strolled down the yellow line, heading toward the far side of the platform. "I was just asking a question," he called out, over his shoulder.

She stomped after him. "Yeah, a question no parent is allowed to answer out loud," she said.

He paused at the place where the platform ended and the tunnel began, unlatching a metal gate that locked up a ladder to the tracks below. "Well, you're not answering it out loud now," he said. "Are you? This is, as you say, all in your head."

"I'm still not answering it," she said.

He started down the ladder. "Oh, you will," he said. "By the end, you will."

She watched him climb down, stepping over the tracks, careful to avoid the third rail, and though she knew that she would follow him—that she *must*—she stood still, holding her ground. She shook her shoulders hard in protest, not wanting to give in, and felt the weight of her guitar case bouncing against her hip for the first time since she'd stepped onto the platform. Had it been there the whole time? She set it down. No use bringing it with her. Serenading him wasn't going to get her out of this.

"Wait up," she said, descending the ladder herself and then following him into the darkness.

2

W hen she saw the light at the end of the tunnel, she did not flinch. The worst that could happen, she figured, was that a train would run her over and send her back to the waking world. And though that would leave her without an answer to the question of what the Salesman was up to, she was sure she'd see him again, that the epiphany he sought to bring her to could be dealt with at a later time.

And so, the train came. But it was riding the track opposite them, so no escape was forthcoming. It hurtled by, faster than any subway car she had ever seen, but that wasn't what stunned her most. What really got her attention was what she saw in the darkness just after it passed by, a fleeting image sprung from the shadows by the train's fading tail lights. She squinted and, almost as if the tunnel could sense what she was doing, overhead lights began to flicker to life. There was a table there, on the other side of the tracks, and chairs, a whole kitchen. She knew this place. And she knew the girl sitting at the table, the girl with the slap bracelets and the *Ride the Lightning* t-shirt, the girl staring at the overturned glass bottle that lay in front of her.

Veronica stumbled backward in disbelief, tripping over a rail as she did and then realizing, as she fell, that the third rail was behind her, that the end was coming now, just as she'd seen something worth seeing, worth exploring. But when she landed, it was not on the hard metal of subway tracks, nor on gravel or wood chips or whatever it was that lay beneath those things, but on the cold linoleum of her parents' kitchen floor.

The Salesman hovered by her side, offering a hand to help her up, a hand that she did not take. "What do you see here?" he asked. "Which night is this?"

She pushed herself up from the floor, her gaze locked on the young girl, the girl she had once been. "Fuck," she said. "This is the night I got pregnant." She looked out the kitchen window, just to make sure, and there was the snow, just as she remembered it.

Not able to bear the sight of the flakes falling, she stared back at the bottle. It was a wine cooler, the brand her mother drank, and that night it was one of only four bottles sitting amidst a castle of empty cans. The boy who had plucked it from the countertop laughed at her as he'd set it down on the table. And then he had stopped laughing, and he had said, "Silver, you are a total lightweight."

It was the first time that alcohol had ever passed between her puckered teenage lips, the first time that *any* of the girls at the table had been liquored up. Veronica watched her younger self duck her head and avert her eyes. This wasn't Vern's fault—Vern, that's what they'd called her then—but she didn't know enough not to feel guilty. Aside from the blizzard, which had stranded her parents somewhere in the wilds of Maine, this was all the boys' fault. They were the ones who had crashed the party, who had broken the tradition.

Veronica looked around the table, at the bodies that had filled the once-empty room. Then she looked at the Salesman, who was still standing beside her, his gaze shifting between Veronica and the scene playing out before them.

"What was the tradition?" he asked her, reading her mind.

Since middle school, when Vern had finally been allowed to stay up and watch the ball drop, her New Year's Eve sleepover had become something of an institution. Vern and her two best friends would crowd around the kitchen table, binge on Chinese food with her parents, and then pile into the four-poster upstairs with a bowl of popcorn, a box of tissues, and a stack of Julia Roberts tapes from the rental place down the street. That was how things were supposed to go. Amy's hands were not supposed to be massaging the crotch of some flat-topped Neanderthal— one was supposed to be entwined with Vern's hand, the other with Desiree's. And Desiree wasn't supposed to be wearing some random guy's letterman's jacket to keep warm; she was supposed to be curled up under the covers, her body balled up against Vern's. They were supposed to watch movies until the bowl of popcorn was empty, or their tear ducts were dry, whichever came first. And then they were supposed to fall asleep beside each other under the heavy down comforter, under the soft cotton sheets. They were supposed to be drinking Diet Coke, not Coors Light. They were supposed to be playing a board game, not Spin the Bottle.

"Supposed to, supposed to, supposed to," said Amy.

"Was I mumbling out loud again?" asked Vern.

Amy extricated one of her hands and set it atop the over-turned wine cooler. "Rules were meant to be broken," she said, giving the bottle a spin.

"We can leave," said Desiree's Letterman.

Amy's Neanderthal nodded. "Buncha other parties'd be glad to have us."

Vern ignored them and stared at the spinning bottle. She watched it as a kitten might watch a game of tennis, her eyes moving in circles as its spin grew slower and slower. If Amy wanted to break the rules, that was fine. Vern just wished that the girl would take these interlopers and make trouble somewhere else.

The truth, Veronica remembered, as the sound of the glass vibrating against the hardwood grew louder and louder, was that this was the night she'd finally had enough of Amy's shenanigans. Ever since her first encounter with the generous johnson of her barbarous Neanderthal, Amy had become singularly obsessed with sex, and not with having it as much as possible—she'd only 'done it' once—but with *talking* about it as much as she could. She asked which kind of dick Vern and Des liked best, knowing full-well that Vern, at least, had never even seen a penis, let alone handled one. She talked constantly about orgasms, about how the one she'd had with the Neanderthal (or, well, the one she *thought* she'd had) hadn't been quite like the little earthquakes she could muster with her own finger, and about how she'd been plotting and planning to make sure that the next one was much better, how she'd stolen *The Joy of Sex* out of the public library to make sure of it, and how she was leafing through the pages of that old tome every goddamned night. And, worst of all, Amy didn't seem to think she had a problem. But she did have a problem, and the night was being ruined by it.

The long neck of the empty wine cooler swung round to a stop, pointing into the small space between the Neanderthal and his runty cousin, the third wheel that they'd brought along, ostensibly, for Vern's sake. Vern gave Desiree a look. Desiree smiled and shrugged. And then, Amy clapped her hands. "Two for one!" she shouted. "Who's first?"

The Neanderthal punched his cousin in the arm, and the Runt offered up his cheek.

"Go easy on him, Ames," said the Letterman. "Dude's a virgin."

The Runt scoffed. "Am not."

"He ain't no more," said the Neanderthal with a chuckle. "Didn't your mom tell you she took care of that?"

"Good one," said the Letterman, hurling an empty across the table at his friend.

In the shadows, still watching, Veronica shook her head. She turned to the Salesman and asked him, "Were you this much of an idiot when you played football?"

He smirked. "I made these kids look like Road Scholars."

"That's Rhodes," she told him. "Not 'road.'"

"See," he said, still smirking.

At the table, the Runt asked, "Can we get this over with?"

"Absolutely," said Amy, leaning across the table. "You ready?"

The Runt nodded.

"Okay then," said Amy, taking hold of his head and latching onto his cheek with her barracuda's mouth.

The Runt went pink, the Letterman screamed "Get a room," and Desiree said, "Quit it," but it was only when the Neanderthal gave her a sharp smack on the ass that Amy let go.

"My turn," said the Neanderthal.

Amy turned around and grabbed hold of the brute by the back of his neck, then buried his face in her bosom. She straddled him, pulled his face out of her cleavage, and then laid on him the sloppiest French kiss that Vern had ever seen, tongues going everywhere, saliva spreading across cheeks and dripping off of chins, the tip of someone's tongue penetrating the cavern of someone's nostril.

Vern went green and Veronica felt her stomach churn in memory. Maybe part of it was the Chinese food, and maybe some other small part of it was the four wine coolers she'd drunk, but a large part of what was making both the young and the old Veronica sick right now was the sheer *wrongness* of this display, of this show that Amy was putting on. These two, they didn't belong together, except in the crudest of ways, except in that 'insert tab A into slot B' way that all men and women fit together. Before this asshole, Amy had just been another flannel-wearing, clarinet-playing band geek. Before, when she liked a guy, she made him a flower out of tissue paper, doused it in fuzzy peach perfume, and stuck it onto the end of a plastic straw. Now, she did this. Her hormones had convinced her that make-believe roses weren't good enough anymore. It was time to move faster, her body told her. The clock was ticking.

Amy dismounted her boy toy and slipped back into her chair. She took off her flannel, a ratty old thing of her dad's that she never took off nowadays, except for its once-a-week washing, and she asked, "That better?"

"Much," said the Neanderthal.

Amy gulped down the last of her beer, nudged Vern, and said, "Your turn."

She resented having to do this, but she knew that there was no way out. With her hand atop the bottle, she wondered which of these idiots she minded kissing the least. She knew who she wanted to kiss *most*, but boys weren't kissing boys tonight and that probably meant that girls weren't kissing girls. Vern went over the physics in her head, trying to figure out how hard she would have to spin it to get the Runt, the lone college boy, the least of all evils, and then she spun the bottle so hard that it nearly spun off of the table.

She turned to Desiree as it whipped around and around, and Desiree must've mistaken the look on her face for panic, because she offered up a bottle of tequila straight away. It wasn't panic that Vern was feeling, though. It was guilt. This situation, this night, was the latest evidence against her, enough ammunition for any prosecutor to prove that she was just as bad as Amy, just as warped and dishonest with herself. If she were really being true, if she were really being the person she was meant to be, she would have told Desiree why she was so adamant about keeping up the New Year's Eve tradition. She would have told her just how often she'd wanted to kiss her pouty lips, or else she would have just kissed them, not even bothering to ask. That would have been the most honest thing to do.

It all went back so far, this lying. Veronica could still recall, clear as day, the moment it became obvious to her who she was. There, in her mind's eye, she saw Desiree strolling in and out of the surf at Red River Beach, down the Cape, a creature positively transformed in the two weeks since the end of school. There was something about her hair swirling gently in the sea-breeze, and something about her face too, something about the thin eyebrows, the green eyes, the high cheeks, something that seemed different than before. Maybe it was just the bikini, a skimpy string thing that the girl was nearly spilling out of, but Veronica couldn't help but stare at Desiree's breasts, which put Veronica's own endowments to shame. Veronica could still feel the heat building as her friend drew closer, a feeling that had never come from thinking about boys, the way her mother had told her it would. She remembered how she'd pulled her legs tighter together, hoping to stave off the sensation, and how that only seemed to make things worse.

But then, suddenly, she was back in the moment, back in the cold of her kitchen, drawn back by the hooting and hollering. She watched—and felt, yes *felt*, because she was no longer watching; she was there, in the seat, inside of the girl she had once been—a soft hand slip over her own.

"Let's just get it over with," said Desiree.

Every eye was on them. Veronica looked down at the table to see what had happened. She looked down to see, and she saw, but she didn't believe, *could not* believe.

"It ain't two out of three," said the Neanderthal.

"Yeah," said the Letterman. "In case you were wondering.

"No," said Veronica. "Sorry. Just spaced."

"You ready then?" said Desiree.

Veronica nodded. "Sure," she said.

Desiree leaned across the corner of the table that sat between them, knocking over the now empty bottle of Pepe Lopez that was in front of her. "You look nervous," she said, giggling, brushing a strand of fallen hair out of Veronica's eyes.

"I do?" said Veronica. *Of course I do*, she thought.

From the shadows came the voice of the Salesman. "Why were you nervous?" he said.

The room disappeared. The table was still there, and the chairs, but the people were gone, and all around her was nothing but darkness.

The Salesman came closer and asked again, "Why were you nervous?"

"Why was I nervous?" she said.

The Salesman sat down in the chair opposite Veronica, and as he did another memory flashed to life around them, then dimmed. She wondered suddenly about who had the power here. Was he the one conjuring these scenes, or was she? Could she force him to see, the way he had just forced her?

"I'll show you why I was nervous," she said, gambling. "It was another night," she said, "around another table."

Veronica picked up the bottle and tossed it to him. "You were there," she said.

As he caught the bottle, it transformed from clear glass to brown.

"Yeah," she said. "You were there and I, I was there." She pointed to her right, to another chair, and the Vern of her memory stepped out of the shadows, a game board under her arm. She sat and began to set it up.

Veronica stayed where she was, remembering who had been there, and she wondered how far she could push the magic of this place. "And Matt," she said, "my brother, your son—he was here." Veronica looked down at her hands, but they were no longer hers. Her engagement ring was gone, her wedding band too, and the fingernails she saw were not bitten, no longer covered in chipped and fading paint. The nails were immaculate now, in fact. The fingers slender and clean, if a bit hairy. Her hands had become her brother's. She looked down and saw that she was wearing the Kimball College shirt Matt that had been wearing that day. All of her had become all of him.

The Salesman shuffled back and forth in his seat, obviously uncomfortable at the sight of Veronica's transformation. He hadn't expected to see his son this night. Hadn't expected it, and wasn't prepared. He looked away, ashamed. "And then what?" he said.

Veronica watched as the dining room of her grandfather's house on Cape Cod materialized around her. As far as the Silver family went, you knew it was the end of summer when the board games came out. It was tradition on the last night down the Cape to gather for a game of Monopoly, or Risk, or Clue. She looked to her left, as the kitchen table of her parents' house elongated into the dining room table at Grampy's, and she noted, with a choked back tear, the old man who appeared next to her father. Grampy hadn't played in years by that point, since before Grammy died, but he stayed up to watch.

"Do you remember this?" Veronica asked the Salesman.

He picked up his cards from the table and mumbled. "I'd rather I didn't."

Then, as young Vern moved the token for Miss Scarlet across the board and began to consult her detective's notepad, Grampy spoke, asking the question that would ruin everything.

"What's the name of that colored fellow who's got his own talk show now?"

"That's Arsenio Hall," someone said.

The Salesman chimed in, laughing as he observed, "Next thing you know, they'll be replacing Carson with a fag. Or a lesbian."

Veronica remembered all too well the words her brother spoke next, so she spoke them. Under her breath, just as he had. "Yeah," she mumbled. "Someone like me."

Vern kicked Veronica under the table and gave her a frown.

So Veronica reached under the table and gave her leg a rub.

Then she pressed on, just as Matt had, just as older brothers often did, deciding that a little sister's discomfort was more than enough reason to keep at it. "Hey Gramp," she said, "didn't Great Aunt Dottie have an affair with another woman once?"

Grampy sighed. "My sister was a wild stallion. She did a lot of things." He reached his hand across the table and patted Veronica's. "But we loved her regardless."

Young Vern set her cards down and said, "I'm going to suggest Mrs. Peacock, in the study—"

Veronica picked Matt's blue pawn up, then set it down in the study beside Vern's piece. Then she spoke the words of her brother once more: "You don't have a comment on all this, sis? You just want to move straight to the accusations?"

"I'm *suggesting* at the moment. I'm not sure yet."

"What weapon?" Veronica asked.

"The rope," said Vern.

Veronica grunted. "I'm not man enough for the gun?"

"That has nothing to do with it."

Calmly, Veronica asked, "Are you trying to say that I'm just a little bitch who'd have to use a rope to kill someone? That I'm some kind of nancy boy?"

Vern frowned. "That's not what I'm—"

"Hey," Veronica shouted at the Salesman, who was sipping at his beer again, "what if Vern's right? What if I am some gay little nancy boy?"

"My son?" the Salesman scoffed. "The Eagle Scout? The star shortstop for the Lions? A faggot?" he spat. "I don't think so."

"What if I told you," said Veronica, "that the reason I keep going back to Wa-Tut-Ca each summer is because I have a crush on the quartermaster?"

"You better cut the shit," said the Salesman.

"Grampy knows," said Veronica, waving a hand toward the old man. "He's known for a long time. You think he was gullible enough to accept that I had a sudden interest in cars, after years of avoiding the garage like the plague? No, he actually asked me questions. He pretended like he gave a damn."

"The quartermaster?" the Salesman shouted. "The Italian kid with the cars? Are you trying to tell me that when you were sleeping over there... Are you trying to tell me that—"

"Yeah," said Veronica. "That's just what I'm trying to tell you. He taught me more than just knots and camping and canoeing and cars. He taught me fellatio and rimming and—"

"Matt!" shouted Vern.

"And anilingus," said Veronica. "He helped me earn my merit badge in anal—"

The Salesman reached across the table and grabbed hold of Veronica's neck with both hands, seeing not his daughter but the son she was pretending to be. Through her tears, Veronica could see Grampy and her Uncle Albert wrapping themselves around the Salesman's hulking arms, trying to pull him off. But she was fading out. She couldn't breathe. Bursts of light were flashing before her eyes, like miniature fireworks announcing the beginning of some grand event, or the end. And then, without realizing what she was doing, she pursed her lips and spat out what little saliva she could muster.

The Salesman let go and stepped away from her. He stared and seemed to see, seemed to see what he had done and who he had done it to. Veronica rubbed at her throat and laughed a mirthless laugh as her old man retreated into the shadows.

3

Veronica stood her ground as the scene shifted around her, as Grampy's dining room disappeared and her parents' kitchen materialized once more. She stared into the shadows, waiting for the Salesman to return, because she could not bear to look at what was about to happen behind her, because this particular tableau was etched onto the insides of her eyelids. This scene was what she saw when she tried to sleep, what she'd been seeing for nearly a decade now, whenever she closed her eyes, whenever rest would not come.

"You wanted to know why I was nervous?" she shouted. "You wanted to know why, old man. That night—what you did to Matt —that's why!"

His voice came from behind her, from the opposite side of the table. "But still you kissed her," he said, meaning to make her turn, to make her see. "Despite the nerves," he said, "you still did it."

"And what good did it do me?" she said, as she turned around to watch, as she gave him the satisfaction of watching her discomfort.

Desiree tilted her head and leaned in, her face drifting toward Vern's like a luxury liner coming into port. Vern closed her eyes.

She blushed as their lips met. Veronica remembered the feeling of shame coursing down through the trunk of her body, the feel of it settling down into that part of her which was crying out for more. Desiree's lips were smooth and thick and warm, and Veronica remembered wanting to die right there, with that feeling the last thing on her mind. But Desiree was going further, feeding off of the energy of the audience, pushing Vern's lips apart with her slippery tongue. Veronica could still remember the taste: tequila and cherry lip gloss.

Alcohol and hormones conspired against them, raging through their bodies, shouting orders. Vern pulled Desiree closer and let herself go. *To hell with all of them*—that's what she'd thought. If it was a show they wanted, then it was a show they were going to get.

Vern's fingers wandered through the tangled curls atop Desiree's head, her other hand running along her friend's back, its gentle arch. One of the boys gave a wolf whistle. Desiree's hands squeezed Vern's shoulders, then ventured southward until they rested above her throbbing heart.

Veronica watched the tears welling up in the eyes of her younger self, recalled how her whole face ached from having to hold them back. Nobody could know what this meant to her. None of these people would understand. And what would Desiree do if she did know, if she felt a tear on her face that she knew wasn't her own? She would disappear, wouldn't she? That's what any sensible straight girl would do, wasn't it?

A bedroom door slammed shut, somewhere down the hall. And then, they parted. Amy and her beau were gone. The Letterman stood then, put his hands on Desiree's shoulders. And Veronica watched as Vern came to the realization that it was over, the night and the dream that she and Desiree would lose together that part of themselves which had so far remained unfound, hidden. Veronica watched a pained smile form on the face of her younger self. She watched as Vern realized that a part of Des would forever belong to the Letterman now, another patch to sew onto his godforsaken jacket. Des gave Vern's hand a squeeze, and then she was gone. Veronica and Vern, the both of them, they watched Desiree slink down the hallway. They listened to the sound of another bedroom door closing, to the sound of a heavy jacket falling to the floor. Then they turned back to the situation at hand.

At the far end of the tunnel, again on the opposite track, there was a light growing brighter. Another train on its way. The Salesman turned to see it and then seemed to spot something: the train's headlamp had illuminated. He stepped toward the nearest pillar and reached behind it. And, as he did, he said, "Could you think of no other reason to stop yourself? Sure, you'd been spurned by love," he said, pulling from the shadows, impossibly, the guitar case she'd left on the platform. "But was there no other place you could take solace?"

"Music?" said Veronica.

"Music," said the Salesman.

Veronica laughed, raising her voice to compete with the volume of the oncoming train. "Christ," she said. "I was a teenager. I had an itch, and my guitar wasn't going to scratch it."

The Salesman shook his head, then shook the guitar at her. "Some itches never stop itching," he said. "Some itches are best left unscratched."

"What the fuck does that even mean?" said Veronica. And then, she caught on. "Wait a minute," she said. "Wait just a damned minute. Are you the one that regrets me having the baby?"

The train was almost upon them now, so it was hard to tell if he was shouting because he was angry, or just because he wanted to be heard. He said, "This is and has always been about you, not me. If I regret anything, it's that your actions forced me to force you into a situation that—"

"My actions?!" she shouted, shoving him. "MY ACTIONS?!" she shouted again, pushing him across the divider between the tracks, right into the light of the train's headlamp.

The train roared as they fell into the light, but then the light changed. It faded, transformed, from bright white to pale purple glow. The guitar tumbled to the floor of what Veronica suddenly realized was a hospital room. And the Salesman, he tumbled into a chair that sat beside a bed. And in that bed, holding a baby, holding *her* baby, was young Vern, who said, with a note of concern in her voice, "Dad?"

"I know," said the Salesman, "that you're unhappy about the situation."

"That's not what I..." said Vern, trailing off. She laughed, then continued: "Yeah, what's there to be unhappy about."

"You stay with us a year," said the Salesman. "We'll help you take care of the baby, you and Tim will have time to get to know each other better, and at the end of the year I'll set you up with an apartment in Boston and you can get on with Berklee like you want to."

Veronica watched herself boiling over, a poisonous mixture of teenage angst and righteous indignation churning inside of her. Vern said, "When will I have time for Berklee with a baby to take care of? And a husband to take care of? A husband, Dad! Are you really going to force me to marry—"

The Salesman stood and set his hands upon Vern's shoulders. "We'll work something out for the baby," he said. "A nanny, or something."

"But what about—"

The Salesman started for the door. "You've done good," he said, not looking at her. "You've done everything I've asked you to do, and you deserve to be repaid for that. For your loyalty," he said, opening the door. "For your understanding," he said, leaving.

"My loyalty?" said Vern. "Ha! And my understanding?" She shook her head and then, a grin playing across her lips, obviously amused by something—Veronica felt strange, not remembering what that something might have been—Vern began to rap. "Boys are stupid," she spit, "boys are dumb. I hate dem boys so much, I kick 'em in da bum. Girls are purty, girls are sweet. Everything 'bout my girl is wicked fucking neat."

In the shadows, Veronica laughed. But Vern, she looked mortified.

"I didn't swear in front of my baby," said Vern, standing up as the baby began to cry. "Nope. Didn't happen."

The baby cried again, and Veronica felt that all too familiar feeling of being split in two, one part of her still standing in the shadows, the other part swaddled up and fussy despite her best efforts. It was a strange feeling, but not an altogether unpleasant one. The unpleasant parts were always really unpleasant—from the toe-curling pain that had come when the baby had first latched onto her breast to the time, at age 7, when her not-so-little one had flown over the handlebars of her bicycle. But, for the most part, she felt this cleaving of herself to be a natural and welcome thing. That part of her that they had pulled from her body, that she had given a name of its very own—it was the first thing she had ever really finished. Her notebooks were full of verses without choruses, of choruses without verses, but this Tracy, this tiny being she had created almost entirely on her own —she was a full song, a full album's worth of songs. And Veronica was prouder of her Tracy than she was of any chord progression she'd plunked out on the piano, than any string of notes she'd noodled out of her guitar.

Vern was trying to sing the baby to sleep now. "Oh, Desiree," she sang, and the baby seemed to respond. "You like that, huh?" said Vern, a smile lightening her weary face. "Oh, Desiree," she sang again. "So long hoped for, so long denied. Please come and rescue my baby and I."

Veronica crept closer to the edge of her memory, wanting to see Tracy's face, suddenly possessed with the desire to see if the baby really was the sweet cherub she remembered, or if it might be the wrinkled old man she feared.

"Des," said Vern, speaking in Veronica's direction. "Is that you?"

Veronica looked down at herself and saw that the chest she had always envied was now obscuring the paunch she had come to dread. Desiree's maroon field hockey number was emblazoned there, on a white shirt. She ran hands along the pleated skirt she had never worn, except in her daydreams, and then she twirled a strand of curly hair around her finger as she said, "Yeah."

"I got your flowers," said Vern, pointing to the shelf by the window. "They were beautiful."

"Were?" said Veronica. "They're dead already, huh?"

Vern teared up a little. "I can't even keep a plant alive," she said. "Pathetic, huh? What makes me think—"

Veronica ran to Vern's side and took hold of her free hand. "Don't," she said. "You'll be an awesome mom. You'll be perfect. And I'll be there, Vern. Best friends for life, right?"

Vern pulled away, headed for the window.

"What?" said Veronica. "Did your dad say something?"

Vern turned around to face Veronica again. To face Desiree again, Veronica had to remind herself. "Never mind," said Vern. "I just... I want to tell you something, something important, but..."

"But what?" said Veronica.

"Never mind," said Vern. "Can you get me out of here?"

"Can you leave?" said Veronica. "What about the baby?"

"I've got the car seat," said Vern. "I've got everything ready."

"But what about the Runt?" said Veronica, looking around the room. "Shouldn't you wait for—"

"I'll just leave him a note," said Vern, handing the baby to Veronica, then rushing across the room for pen and paper. "Tracy and I just want to be with you right now. Just us girls. Can you do that?"

Veronica looked down into the face of her daughter. *Damn it*, she thought. *Wrinkled old man.*

"Desiree?" said Vern.

"Hell yeah," said Veronica, strapping Tracy into the car seat. "Let's go."

Vern did a little dance and gave a little *squee*, then grabbed the handle of the car seat and stepped through the door. Veronica made to follow after her, but a hand squeezed her arm and stopped her in her tracks. She turned and saw the Salesman. She looked down at herself and saw her own small tits were back. *Damn*, she thought.

"So," said the Salesman, as the hospital room faded away, "where did you go that day?"

"Hampton," said Veronica. "The beach."

"With a baby?" said the Salesman.

"I was seventeen," she told him, shrugging him off. "And you'd trapped me. Can you blame me for trying to escape?"

"No," said the Salesman, circling her, "but why is it that, whenever you tried, you failed?"

"I didn't try that often," said Veronica. "I was a good girl."

The Salesman laughed. "A good girl?" he said. "What about that play your brother wrote about you and your, uh, exploits?"

Veronica blushed, looked down at her feet. "That play wasn't about me," she said.

"Oh, he may have embellished a little," said the Salesman, "but it was about you. I may be slow, sweetheart, but I ain't that slow."

"It wasn't about me," said Veronica, noting that, out of the darkness, a familiar pair of buildings were emerging. It was her grandfather's house, in the years after his death, when the family was still deciding what to do with it. The paint job on the barn was half-finished, the sign that had once read 'Garage' replaced with one that read 'The Theatre.'

"It wasn't about you?" said the Salesman, leading her toward the barn's open doors. "Then what about the way you and Desiree looked at each other on opening night, when we all went to see it?"

He extended a hand, which she took, and he led her inside.

❧ 4 ❧

She could not recall taking a seat, nor sitting through her brother's tedious curtain speech, nor even the first two-thirds of the show. One moment, they were at the door, the next the play was reaching its climax.

And Veronica was torn, not sure which drama the Salesman had brought her here to witness: the farce playing on stage or the romance playing out in the seats. The Salesman had found them a place opposite Vern and Desiree, the stage thrust between them, but that didn't clear things up at all. The way the actors stood, the way the scenes played out, Veronica could always see her younger self off in the distance. She felt a headache coming on as she struggled to focus on foreground and then background, background and then foreground.

There was a single young woman on stage now, a blonde in her early 20s—cast first and foremost, Veronica remembered, because her hair was the opposite color of Vern's. The character she was playing, according to the photocopied program Veronica consulted, was Nica, and she was shouting.

"No!" Nica called to someone offstage. "You can't. You can't do that! You can't! You're a... and he... he..."

And then, there came a knocking, not from the door Nica was shouting at, but from another on the other side of the stage.

"What now?" grumbled Nica.

"Chinese food!" said the woman at the door.

Nica did not cross to welcome the delivery person. Instead, she remained focused on what was happening behind door number one. "I didn't order any Chinese food," she said.

"The order was placed by a gentleman by the name of Tim."

In her seat, Veronica laughed. That name hadn't been changed to protect the innocent now, had it? Then again, was the Runt really innocent? Of anything?

Nica continued her watch at door number one as she called back, over her shoulder, "All right. Come in. Door's open."

Onto the stage walked a young woman wearing Birkenstocks, a flannel, and an Ani DiFranco t-shirt. Veronica laughed at the lazy stereotype, then noted her brother's one attempt at original-ity: a backwards baseball cap from Intercourse, Pennsylvania that he had picked up on a family trip to that state's largest auto show the year their grandfather died. But she was sure it didn't mean anything beyond the connotation that the girl was loose and a lesbian. Her brother was inscrutable, yes, but he was also shallow and incapable of nuance.

"You're not Chinese," said Nica, sizing up the delivery person —Andi, according to the program.

"You're quick," said Andi.

"And you just lost your tip," said Nica, rifling through the pockets of her denim mini-skirt. "Cash only, I suppose?"

"Actually," said Andi, "the order was prepaid on your..."

"Fiancé?"

"Yes," said Andi, setting an enormous brown paper bag down upon the living room table. "Your fiancé's credit card. I just need him to sign a copy of the receipt and I can get out of here."

Nica slumped into an armchair. "You'll have to wait a couple of minutes," she said, gesturing to door number one. "He's in the bedroom, fucking my best friend."

"Interesting relationship," said Andi.

"You're telling me," said Nica.

Beside Veronica, the Salesman held up his hands, and all else stopped. Veronica looked out at the stage, at the audience. They were all frozen in place. She stared at Vern and Desiree. They were holding hands now, on the sly. Not even hands, really. Just fingers, one hooked around another.

The Salesman tapped her on the shoulder. "Did Desiree ever actually sleep with Tim?" he asked.

"No!" said Veronica. "I told you, this isn't about—"

The Salesman shushed her, clapped his hands once, and everyone around them came back to life.

On stage, Nica asked Andi, "You want a drink?"

Andi said, "I don't turn 21 until October."

"Never stopped me," said Nica.

"And I'm driving," said Andi.

"Okay," said Nica. "Whatever."

From behind door number one came a comic moan and the creaking of a bed frame.

"So," said Andi, "is every Friday like this around here?"

"What do you mean?" said Nica.

Andi opened the bag as she spoke, pulling from it a white box and chopsticks. "I mean," she said, "does your fiancé sleep with your best friend every Friday night?"

"No," said Nica, tucking her knees up under her chin and running her hands over her purple leggings. "This is the first time. He's usually faithful. And she's usually gay."

"Oh," said Andi.

There came again then the sound of coming, or at least the farcical approximation of that sound. The offstage voices hollered clichés, took the Lord's name in vain, thanked Him for their pleasure, and then trailed off.

Nica leapt to her feet, stalked over to the door, and stared at it for a moment, before turning around to face Andi once more. She jammed a thumb between her teeth.

"What?" said Andi, slurping lo mein into her mouth.

Nica looked over her shoulder as she tapped her foot on the floor. Then she blurted out, "You want to fuck?"

"Excuse me?" said Andi, setting down box and chopsticks and eyeing the door.

"Do you want to sleep with me?" said Nica. "I wanna make them sorry. Maybe if they come out here and see me with you, they'll think twice about screwing with me again. So, do you want to?"

"Uh," said Andi, checking her watch. "I couldn't."

"Why?" said Nica, clutching her hands together behind her back and thrusting her chest upwards and outwards, like a good soldier, as if to make the other girl see what she was missing. "Do you think I'm ugly?" she said as she drew closer.

"No," said Andi. "I, uh, think you're very attractive."

Nica stepped behind Andi and slipped off her hat. "Then what's the problem?" she said as she ran her fingers through the other girl's curly locks.

"Well," said Andi, "you're not exactly my type."

Nica set her fingers to work on Andi's neck as she pulled her face close to Andi's ear. "Ah," she said, brushing her lips against Andi's cheek. "but you most certainly are my type."

Andi leapt up and away, stumbling. "Do you have a penis?" she said.

Nica giggled, then stopped, and then, finally, understood. "You mean you're a... No, you can't be. This is just... You're straight?"

"I told you you weren't my type."

"Wait," said Nica, flabbergasted. "You, in the Ani shirt and the flannel and the... the... You're straight?"

Andi sighed. "I tried to tell you."

"I don't believe this!" Nica shouted to the heavens as she

slumped again into her chair. "Am I doing something wrong here?"

"No," said Andi. "I just happen to like dick."

In the audience, Veronica moved to get up, saying "I'm not watching this anymore," but she was startled back to her seat by two things. First, the Salesman's hand on her arm. And second, the sight, across the way, of Vern and Desiree mirroring them.

"Sit down," the Salesman told Veronica. "Sit down," Vern told Desiree.

And now, with the rest of the room on mute, Veronica could hear Vern say to Desiree, "I'm not embarrassed. Why are you embarrassed?"

"You wouldn't understand," said Desiree.

The Salesman raised a finger to his lips and all sound disappeared again, save the words being spoken on stage. Andi and Nica were both seated now, sitting on either side of the living room table, passing the box of lo mein between them.

"Do you throw yourself at delivery people often?" said Andi.

"I throw myself at just about everybody I get a chance to," said Nica.

"And why's that?"

"Because I can't be with the person I want to be with," said Nica.

Veronica stared across the way, listening to the play, but watching something else. Vern and Desiree were no longer holding hands. They sat only inches apart, but those inches might just as well have been miles.

"Okay," said Andi. "So, who do you want to be with?"

"My best friend," said Nica.

Andi gestured to door number one. "The one who's back there?"

"Yes."

"But why?" said Andi.

"I don't know," said Nica. "I guess because she completes me."

Andi scoffed, "You've seen *Jerry Maguire* one too many times."

"What?" said Nica.

"You haven't seen it yet?" said Andi. "You're not missing much. Anyway, that's what the fucking pretty boy Tom Cruise says to that Zellweger chick at the end of the movie."

"What have you got against Tom Cruise?" said Nica.

"Honey, I could write a book about what I've got against Tom Cruise."

"Okay," said Nica. "What's your point?"

"My point," said Andi, "is that you saying she 'completes' you is a bunch of bullshit. The only person who ever completes you is you. And putting that pressure on someone else... Man, that's some fucked up shit. God, do you know how many unoriginal, over-sappy, under-attractive men have tried to use that one on me since that movie came out?"

"A lot?" said Nica.

Andi stood, working herself up, stalking back and forth between her chair and the edge of the stage as she spat the rest of her monologue. "You bet your ass," she said. "I say, to hell with all this completion crap. Just come straight out and say you want to fuck and get it over with. The direct approach is so much more honest, and so much easier to deal with. If more men came up to me and said shit like, 'Nice shoes. Wanna fuck?' instead of this 'You complete me' bullshit, I'd be giving head a lot more often."

"Well," said Nica, pausing as the audience roared with laughter, "thank you for that insight."

"You're welcome," said Andi, sitting, flush from her speech. "Now, back to the problem at hand. You want to be with your best friend, but your fiancé is the one keeping a roof over your head."

"Actually," said Nica, "it's my dad who's paying the bills right now, though Tim has all these prospects, or something. Or so they tell me."

"Well, whatever," said Andi, gesturing to door number one

again. "Those two have been off doing their thing for a long time now. Your fiancé and your friend," said Andi, "not your fiancé and your dad, of course. And they're going to keep doing their thing. The real question is, when are you going to start doing your thing, and when are you going to realize that whoever comes along for the ride is just—"

Veronica leapt to her feet and shouted "STOP!" and the audience was gone, the theater empty, except for the two actors on stage.

Nica and Andi cast glances at the Salesman, as if looking for instructions. Veronica turned to look at him herself and saw him nod them off. By the time Veronica looked at the stage again, they were gone.

The Salesman stood and made his way toward the door.

"It doesn't matter who's along for the ride?" said Veronica, stomping after him. "I'm no romantic, but that's a pretty fucking bleak outlook on love."

The Salesman shook his head as he stepped outside.

Veronica followed him, stumbling as she stepped out, not onto grass as she'd expected, but back onto the subway tracks.

"Why do you place such high stock in Desiree?" said the Salesman. "Why?"

"Do you know how deep it runs between her and me?" said Veronica. "Do you know how far back it goes?"

"To the beach?" he said, a note of disgust in his voice. "To you wet with desire for a girl in a bikini too skimpy for fourteen year old to wear? I see inside your head," he said, tapping a pair of fingers hard against his temple. "I know it all."

"No," she said, searching the darkness for the right place to take him, knowing it must be out there. "It goes back even further than that."

"Really," he said, snorting back a laugh. "Okay then. Show me."

The trains had stopped running for the night, so they made their way there on foot, emerging from the tunnel just outside Kenmore Square, then trekking down Commonwealth Avenue as the sun rose on an empty Back Bay.

"This is eerie," Veronica said to the Salesman as they made the turn near Packard's Corner, "like some movie about the end of the world."

The Salesman pointed to the sky. "No mushroom clouds," he said.

"Not with a bang but a whimper," said Veronica, smiling despite her aching feet.

"That's from *The Stand*," said the Salesman. "Right? From the mini-series they did on ABC?"

"It's from T.S. Eliot."

"Yes," he said, "but it's also from *The Stand*."

Veronica shook her head and sighed. Then she told him, "You're really nothing like him, you know."

"Who?" he said.

"My father," she said. "You're what I wish he was. Like the

second draft of a song," she said, "after I've cut all the shitty parts, or at least most of them. After I've cut it down to three-oh-five."

The Salesman had nothing to say to that. No comment about her Billy Joel reference. No nothing. Whereas the real version, her father out there in the waking world, wouldn't have been able to shut up. Instead, the Salesman just kept on. And kept on keeping on. It wasn't until they got there, to 1325, that the Salesman said another word.

It began with a smirk, something so small she might not have noticed it had she not been staring at him the whole time and waiting for something. Anything.

"What?" said Veronica.

"I made good on my promise, didn't I?"

"Yes," said Veronica, as they started up the stairs. "You did."

"Do you know who used to live here?" asked the Salesman.

Veronica groaned, then decided to play along. "No," she said. "Who?"

"The Bad Boys of Boston," he said. "Aerosmith, that's who! And my brother, your uncle, he opened for them once upon a time."

"Did he now?"

"Sure did," said the Salesman. "Played bass. I think it was up at Canobie Lake, or somewhere around there."

"I never knew that," said Veronica, rolling her eyes, hoping he could not see what she was thinking right then and there.

"At any rate," he said, as they made their way into the apartment, as they blended into the bustling crowd within, "what day is this? What have you brought me here to see?"

Veronica took his hand and brought him into the living room, and then she tucked them away in a corner to watch.

Vern sat on the center of the couch, with Tracy on her lap, as laughing children circled around the two of them, and around the birthday cake that sat on their coffee table. The adults stood around Veronica and the Salesman, on the opposite wall, armed with cameras and camcorders. And as the crowd began to sing "Happy Birthday," Vern huddled close to her daughter. "Make a wish," she told Tracy, as they leaned toward the cake. And then they blew at the candles in unison, smoke blowing back at them, the scent of melting wax in the air.

All around Veronica and the Salesman, there came one flash after another. It felt like overkill, Veronica remembered, like she'd been thrust onto the red carpet of the Grammys in a tattered old set of pajamas. But for Tracy, who at three was already becoming something of a diva, it was heaven. She hammed it up, loving the attention, posing for this camera, and then that one, never noticing, as Vern did, that one of the paparazzi had stopped shooting altogether and had lowered her weapon.

Veronica and the Salesman looked, with Vern, at a frowning Desiree. Vern tilted her head and frowned back, and Des seemed to catch herself then, forcing a big, bright smile onto her face. But Vern knew there was something wrong.

The Runt crept up behind Vern and rubbed at her shoulders, while Tracy leaned forward on Vern's lap to swipe at the cake's frosting with a pair of eager fingers. Across the room, Desiree was slipping through the crowd, past Veronica and the Salesman, down the hallway, toward the bedrooms. And that was when curiosity got the best of Vern. She pulled herself out from under the Runt's grasp, set Tracy down on the couch beside her, and followed after her friend. Veronica took the Salesman by the arm and followed, too.

In the bedroom, Desiree stood by the window. She ran her fingers along the lacy fringe of the curtains that the Runt had picked out on that day, a little over three years before, when Vern had finally told him about the baby, when the size of her paunch had basically forced her to. He'd wanted to celebrate, and so he'd bought curtains at a K-Mart across the parking lot from the McDonalds where they'd been having lunch. "To remember this moment forever," he'd said, showing her the ugly things. And she had remembered. She didn't think her brain would ever let her forget.

"You didn't have to leave the party just to check on me," said Desiree.

Vern rounded the bed and took hold of friend's hand. "Are you okay?" she said.

Desiree turned and faced her, facing also the two onlookers she could not see. Her eyes were swollen and red. She leaned back against the wall, managing a weak smile. "Do you ever think about that night?" asked Desiree. "About New Year's Eve?"

"What about it?" said Vern, holding Desiree's face in her hands, wiping at the tears with her thumbs.

Desiree looked away, looked down. She tapped her fist against the window pane. "It was probably even earlier than that," she said. "Do you remember that canoe trip when we were twelve, when your dad took us way up into Maine?"

Vern nodded. "It was wicked cold."

"And he said, 'If you girls don't want to do this...'"

"But we'd already slipped into our life jackets, had already started arguing about who got which oar."

Desiree smiled. "We were a day into the trip, miles and miles away from the car, and away from civilization. It was so peaceful," she said. "I remember we saw a moose on the side of the river, just grazing."

"And then we hit those rapids," said Veronica, shaking her head.

"I fell overboard," said Desiree. "And it... it gets fuzzy from there. But on New Year's a few years back, when you kissed me, and ever since, I... I've started to remember."

Veronica felt a real physical change in her body then, could see that Vern felt it too, their pulses quickening, chests rising and falling with greater speed. "My dad thought you might have hypothermia," said Vern, picking up the story. "We set up the tents and he told me to go inside, strip us both down, and then to curl up with you in a sleeping bag, to keep you warm."

"For years," said Desiree, "I thought it was just a dream. But it was the safest and best feeling I'd ever had, you pressed up against me, holding me. And when you kissed me on New Year's..."

Vern looked like she was beginning to hyperventilate, and Veronica struggled to breathe right along with her. They inhaled deeply, trying to keep control.

"Calm down," said the Salesman.

"What?" said Vern to Desiree, unable to say more, hoping that Desiree would answer the question, would answer this question that Vern had been asking herself for more years than she could remember.

Desiree grabbed Vern by the back of the neck and pulled her close, pressing her lips to Vern's. And it took a moment for Vern to respond, took almost too long in fact, for Desiree was already pulling away by the time Vern opened her mouth to kiss her back. Suddenly, there were tears streaming down Vern's cheeks, but Veronica couldn't tell—couldn't remember—whether they were Desiree's or her own.

"Do we have to stay?" said the Salesman. "Haven't you proved your—"

But Veronica clapped a hand over his mouth and held him there, wanting him to see, wanting him to see it all.

Fingers tore at the buttons of Vern's blouse till it hung open at her sides. And Desiree seemed surprised that Vern's breasts were bare, though they must've gone shopping together a hundred times, though she must've known what she'd find. Veronica closed her eyes, could feel herself in Vern's body again, could feel Desiree's hands on her. They were uncertain hands, and cold to the touch, but they were soft, and careful, and they felt like they belonged there.

Veronica opened her eyes in time to see Vern pull Desiree away from the wall, in time to see them falling against the bed.

She closed her eyes again as she watched Des's anxious fingers pushing Vern's skirt up, then she felt those fingers slip up along her legs, her thighs, her hips, and then finally, mercifully, to that warmest of places.

The Salesman struggled against her grip and Veronica opened her eyes. She tried to keep the Salesman's mouth shut, to keep him from saying whatever words might stop this. Together, they watched as Vern wrapped her legs around Desiree's back and squeezed, as Vern slipped her own hands underneath Des's turtleneck while a pair of lips pressed hot against her neck.

"ENOUGH!" shouted the Salesman. His voice was muffled by Veronica's fingers, but it was, apparently, clear enough, for everything went black once again, and they began to fall through the darkness.

"Don't you see?" said Veronica, as they dropped. "It could have been her and me! Did you ever even consider that?"

The wind around them was picking up now, as they sped along, but the Salesman's voice boomed over it. "Don't you remember what she said to you?" he said. "Before the baby was born? Don't you remember what she said to you, and where she said it, and where you were going?"

They landed in the back seat of a car, of Desiree's car, just in time to see Vern grab hold of Desiree's forearm and squeeze.

"Pull over," said Vern, closing her eyes, leaning her head back into the soft leather of the Cabrio's passenger seat. "I think I'm going to be sick."

Des flicked on the directional, and they all listened to the thing click and then pause, click and then pause, as they waited to turn. Veronica recalled that moment in *Peter Pan* where Captain Hook begins to hear the ticking and tocking that signal the return of his nemesis, the crocodile, come back to finish what it started with the mauling of his hand. The click of Desiree's direction was like that, these days—every time they turned in somewhere, it was to give Vern a chance to throw up without ruining the upholstery.

The car turned—a little too sharply, Veronica thought, the whole of her body sliding into the Salesman's, the whole of Vern's sliding into Desiree's—and then it rolled to a stop. Veronica stared through the windshield at the red brick and white wood-work of St. Mary's Church. Desiree shifted the car into park, pushing the stick forward with such force that Veronica thought she might break off the handle.

"Why are you so angry?" Vern asked her.

Desiree tapped her lacquered fingernails on the steering wheel.

"I'm feeling sick," said Vern, reaching to turn the heat down and the fan off. "Okay? I'm not fibbing."

Desiree stared down at the dash. "I know you're not fibbing. It's just that, if we could get to the doctor's office and get this over with, we wouldn't have to... *You* wouldn't have to deal with this anymore.

Vern slid her hand underneath her sweater and rubbed at her stomach. She pinched the loose roll of flesh just above the waist-band of her sweats. Veronica remembered how her tummy had never felt so soft before, so pudgy. With her free hand, Vern plucked her can of Chelmsford Ginger Ale from the cup holder, the maroon and yellow aluminum glistening with condensation. The cup holders were positioned right in the path of the heater's vents, and Veronica could still remember the taste of the warm soda, could still remember wishing she hadn't left it there so long.

Desiree glared at Vern, shaking her head.

"What are you looking at me like that for?" asked Vern.

The car shuddered for a moment from the assault of the fierce February wind. Vern twisted the knob for the fan, bringing it back up to full blast.

"You know you're not supposed to eat or drink anything beforehand, don't you?"

"I could throw up all over your car," said Vern, sipping some more of her soda. "Would you prefer that?"

"I'd prefer that we get to the damn doctor's office before you have any more second thoughts."

Vern stared into the mirror on her side. Veronica stared too, watching gray puffs of exhaust rising up from the back of the car. "Second thoughts," Vern mumbled. "I'm on third thoughts now, and fourth thoughts..."

Vern unbuckled her seatbelt and shifted, turning her back to Desiree and leaning her side into the soft leather.

A pair of hands—cold, Veronica remembered—slipped up under the back of Vern's sweater, thumbs kneading at just the right spot. Vern exhaled, let go a low, soft moan.

"Don't you want to be done with this?" asked Desiree.

"It's not that bad," said Vern, grimacing and wincing, though Desiree could not see.

"I mean, why would you even want to have his—"

"It's not his," snapped Vern, twisting herself around. "It's mine."

Desiree slumped back into the driver's seat, rubbed her expert thumbs along her own furrowed brow.

"You know," said Vern. "I was on the phone with the nurse at the doctor's office, listening to all of their instructions—don't eat anything after midnight, bring someone to give you a ride home—and she started to sound like the teacher in Charlie Brown, her voice like an out-of-tune trumpet. But then, at the end, she says this one thing, and it's this one thing I can't get out of my head."

"What did she say?"

"She said, 'After the procedure, we'll remove the products of conception.'"

Desiree turned away, stared out through the windshield at the church's vast parking lot.

Vern clasped her hands over her stomach. "Doesn't that make it sound like they're taking out the garbage?"

"They've got to be clinical about it," said Desiree.

"But what do they even do with it when they're done, Des? Throw it in the trash with the half of their tuna fish sandwich that they couldn't finish? Flush it down the toilet like we did with goldfish when we were kids?" Veronica yelped, "What are they going to do with my baby?"

It was a question that Desiree couldn't answer, or didn't *want* to answer. She sat silent, her hand on the stick shift, waiting for instructions.

"You don't have anything to say?" said Vern, wiping at her eyes, her nose.

Desire wrapped one of her amber curls around a finger and began to twirl it. She bit down on her lower lip, closed her eyes.

Vern swatted at Desiree's hand. "Stop twirling your hair and say what you want to say!"

"You've made your decision, Veronica. What am I supposed to say?"

"I haven't made—"

"Yes," said Desiree. "You have."

"And you think it's the wrong one," said Vern.

Desiree shook her head and shifted the car into gear. "What does it matter, what I think? It doesn't matter," she said. "And it never will."

The Salesman opened his door and slipped out of the car. Veronica thought to stay, hoped they would take her away, but when the car didn't move, when the girls in the front said nothing further, she got out and she stomped over to the Salesman, who was walking toward the tree line, toward the shadows, his work here nearly done.

❦ 6 ❧

Into the woods he went, and into the woods she followed. But they weren't long amongst the trees. Soon enough, the sky darkened over them and all light seemed to fade out of the world. "It did matter," she yelled into the void. "It did!" But he said nothing back.

Out of the darkness then, there came one final flash, and Veronica saw herself climbing into the four-poster, beckoning the Runt to climb on top of her. She felt her soul swoon as he drove himself into her, breaking her open for the first time. She watched Vern wince, her brow furrowed, and she remembered how badly it had hurt, the Runt burying himself into her, the words of her Grampy's motto—"Honesty breeds happiness"—falling away like dust from the drill-hole.

The silence of the scene was eerie, but that was the way it had been. He didn't make any noise at all, the Runt, not even as he squeezed hold of her shoulders, his whole body convulsing against hers, that throbbing, awful piece of him seeping into her.

Neither of them said anything when it was done. He simply lay on top of her. And she, she turned away from him, her eyes focused on the nightstand, squinting, seeing something she was sure she wasn't seeing: the small square he'd taken from his wallet, the package unopened, untorn.

Quiet. It was so quiet that, like in the book her brother had sent her for Christmas, she could hear the snow falling faintly through the universe and, like herself, faintly falling.

The next few weeks were a blur, a video cassette on fast-forward. She watched herself pick up the phone and hang it up, pick it up and hang it up. God, he had called so many times.

And then there was the stainless steel bowl she kept by her bed, the one they used to make pancakes with, the bowl she seemed to fill at least twice a night when the nausea came.

And, of course, there was the trip to her Aunt Michaela's office for the test, a test that a pediatrician in their prim and proper town rarely had to give. All of it was like a blur until that afternoon in Desiree's car, on the way to another doctor's office, on the way to a doctor who would Wite-Out the mistake, who would give her one more chance to pass the final exam of her adolescence. It was all a blur until that moment of truth when she grabbed hold of Desiree's forearm and squeezed, until she asked Des to say what she wanted to say.

Once again, Desiree shook her head and shifted the car into gear. "What does it matter, what I think? It doesn't matter," she said. "And it never will."

Veronica closed her eyes. "It did matter!" she shouted again, into the darkness.

"I know it did," said the Salesman, stepping out of the void and back to her side, a flashlight in his hand.

"It mattered," said Veronica, "because she was the one who held my hair back during every hurried trip to the toilets at school. It mattered because I knew, even then, that she'd be the one holding my hand in the delivery room, the one reminding me to breathe. And it mattered because, even though I knew you were going to force me to marry the Runt, even though it would be his chapped lips that pressed against mine when the preacher said so, and not hers, it was she who I loved. She was my partner. She always has been. She always will be."

"But what a dangerous partner to have," said the Salesman. "Look what she almost made you do."

Veronica jabbed a finger into the Salesman's chest. "She almost made me see that she loved me!" she said. "She almost made me admit that I loved her. And what the hell would have been wrong with that."

"She almost made you kill your daughter."

"Is there a point to all this?" she asked him.

"Always," he said.

"You want me to say it," she said. "You want me to say it out loud."

"Yes," said the Salesman.

Veronica looked down, unable to look him in the eye, or maybe just unwilling. "Okay," she said. "Fine. I wonder. Every once in awhile, I wonder what it would be like if my daughter had never been..."

But she trailed off as she noticed the light rising around her, the subway platform materializing again before her very eyes.

"Yes," he said. "Go on. Had never been what?"

Veronica stared across the platform at her guitar case, sitting there all by its lonesome.

"You know," she said, "in all my time at Berklee, and all the time since, I only ever wrote one song worth keeping, one song worth a damn."

"But that wasn't what you did," said the Salesman. "Your thing was reinventing songs. There was the venomous dirge you made out of 'Here Comes the Hotstepper,' the contemplative cover of 'Freedom '90'—"

"But there was that one song," she said, turning from the guitar to face him.

"Which one?" he said.

"I don't remember much of it," she said. "I wouldn't let

anyone record my originals because, you're right, they weren't my thing. But there was something about it," she said, pausing for a moment to listen to a guitar tuning in the distance, then deciding the sound was just a lie of the mind. "I'm sure the lyrics were dumb," she said, "but the meaning behind them..."

"Was what?" said the Salesman. "What was the meaning?"

"I wrote it for my little girl," she said. "It was a distillation. Of all this stuff, everything I wanted her to know about my mistakes, everything I wanted her to learn from them. And I don't know," she said. "Maybe it didn't work. Maybe it was terrible, but—"

The Salesman pressed a finger to her lips, then nodded over her shoulder. She turned around in time to see Vern begin to play the guitar, an empty pickle jar standing at her feet, a sleeping baby strapped to her back.

"You can't be president," sang Vern. "You can't be the boss. You can't make the rules, cause you don't know the cost."

And then came the chorus, and Veronica sang with her, "So, just sing, Angel. Sing, when you can't do a thing. When you can't do a thing, you just sing, Angel. Sing."

On either side of them, trains rolled into the station, the morning's first commuters making their way. A small crowd gathered as Vern delivered the next verse. "You can't hit that ball," she sang. "You can't make that toss. You can bear a child," she sang, and then she belted, pouring everything she had into the last line, "but you can't bear the cross."

All of them sang the chorus now, Veronica reaching for the Salesman's hand as she did, intending to squeeze it, to thank him for this moment. But he was gone. She whirled about, looking for him amongst the onlookers, but he was nowhere to be found.

Vern finished the song. The crowd showered her with applause and her cup runneth over with tips. Then the people were gone, onto their trains, and then the trains were gone too, and just the two of them remained, Vern and Veronica.

"What are you waiting for?" said Vern, as she packed up her gear.

"What?" said Veronica.

"Which train?" said Vern. "Where are you going?"

Veronica raised an eyebrow. "Are you speaking in metaphors now, too?"

"No," said Vern, emptying the pickle jar of its bills, its change. "I'm just making small talk."

"Oh," said Veronica, confused, wondering if Vern recognized her or not, if this were memory or something stranger. "I, uh, I suppose I'm heading home."

"And where is home?" said Vern.

"You *are* speaking in metaphors, aren't you?"

Vern smirked. "Aren't we all?"

Veronica leaned against a pillar and sighed. "I'm supposed to tell you it's all going to get better, I suppose."

Vern laughed as she picked up the guitar case. "Sure. Maybe," she said. "That'd be a lie, and I'd know it. But that's what we're good at, you and me. So, go ahead."

"Okay," said Veronica. "It's all going to get better."

Vern smiled, then mocked, "You almost sounded convinced."

"I've got years more practice than you," said Veronica.

"True, that. But here's a question for you: better than what?"

"Excuse me?" said Veronica.

"It's going to get better than what?" said Vern, setting her free hand on Veronica's shoulder, looking her dead in the eye.

"Than life right now," said Veronica. "I mean, we're going to leave the Runt."

"I know we are," said Vern. "It's a matter of time. But that's just going to be different, right? Not better."

"Life without the Runt is way better than—"

"For you," said Vern, shaking her head and walking away. "But what about for Tracy?" she said, reaching a hand behind her back to rub the sleeping infant. "What about for your daughter? What is life going to be like for her, without her dad around?"

"I'll still be there," said Veronica. "And Desiree, too. And there are plenty of men in our life to play the father figure if she needs one. My brother, my cousin Michael. Things will get better, as she gets used to it."

"And when she gets used to it," said Vern, "what then? You don't think something else will come up? What about puberty for her, middle-age for you?"

"Watch it," said Veronica, offended.

"What about the stress of trying to cram all the years you should have spent with Desiree into the few years you have left?"

Veronica sighed. "Things will never get better," she said. "Is that your point?"

"No," said Vern, exasperated. "My point is that things are just things, that life is just life. It's never better or worse. It just is. And the sooner you realize that, the sooner you remember that—"

Veronica pulled herself out of her slouch, pulled herself away from the pillar that was holding her tired body upright. "Remember that?" she said. "Remembering that implies that I ever thought that to begin with."

"You have," said Vern. "In the quiet moments. In the, for lack of a better word, 'best' moments."

Veronica ran a hand over Vern's cheek. "When did I lose you?" she said. "When did I lose this part of myself, this hopeful, smiling part?"

Vern took Veronica's hand in her own. "You didn't," she said. "I'm still here."

"So," said Veronica. "What do I do?"

Vern stomped over to the station's exit. "To begin with," she said, pointing up the stairs with the guitar case, "you stop waiting for the piano of death to fall on your head. Instead, you leap up into the air to meet that son of a bitch and you play the shit out of it until you both come crashing down together!"

Veronica chuckled. "Did you just mix your metaphors?" she said.

"Hellifiknow," said Vern. "Our brother was the English major, remember? We just write silly pop songs," she said, crossing to stand in front of Veronica once more. "Don't ever think too hard about what they mean, or they'll stop meaning anything."

Vern set the guitar case between them, then pushed it gently into Veronica's hands. She gave her older self a bear hug and a peck on the cheek, and then she ran for the stairs.

Veronica slung the guitar case over her shoulder and followed the lead of the girl she had once been, the woman she would strive to be again.

❧ II ❧
BETTER OFF THAN THE
WIVES OF DRUNKARDS

JULY 2000–APRIL 2001

he roller coaster came to a full and complete stop just after they'd slid past the loading area and the control booth, just as they'd descended the small slope that would take them into the ride proper. Ahead of their train, Veronica saw the tunnel of pulsing blue lights grow suddenly dark. She heard the sounds of the Space Mountain "energy surge" fade into silence. And then she turned around in her seat, as best she could with the T-bar restraint keeping her in place, and she asked her cousin, "What the hell is going on here?"

Michael shrugged and said, "Dunno."

The overhead lights came on, washing out the attraction's eerie ambience. A few moments later, one of the ride attendants came bouncing down the set of stairs just to the left of their vehicle, a heretofore invisible set of steps which descended down the slope and into the now bright white light of the tunnel.

"What's going on?" cried Veronica to the attendant.

"Nothing to be worried about, ma'am," he said with a smile. "You'll be on your way shortly."

Veronica groaned.

"Chill out," said Michael. "I'm sure they'll figure it out soon."

Veronica held her left arm up, twisted her wrist back and forth. "You see what time it is, Michael?"

"Oh, Jiminy Cricket," said Michael. "Not the damn schedule again."

"We're supposed to be leaving for the next park in twenty minutes, and we haven't even gotten in line for Dumbo yet, let alone ridden the stupid thing."

"If you were that concerned about Tracy getting to ride flying elephants, why didn't you have Des and Jenna take her over there while we were in here?"

"Because I want to see her on the ride," said Veronica. "You don't understand, Michael. Getting your kid on all the rides she wants to ride is only part of it. The other part, the bigger part, is being there to watch her enjoy them. That's what makes the interminable flight and the hellish heat and the exorbitant price of the watered-down soda all worth it. Otherwise, what's the point?"

"I think the point is to enjoy yourself," said Michael. "If you didn't want to ride this ride, we could've—"

Veronica turned her head to look him in the eye as best she could. "I wanted to ride Space Mountain, Michael. It was the one thing I wanted to do for myself. I've told you that."

"Okay," said Michael. "I'm just saying... If you wanted to do Dumbo instead, we could've come back another—"

Veronica sighed and turned away from him again.

"What is it about Space Mountain anyway?" asked Michael. "You've avoided every other thrill ride in the place."

This was true, Veronica thought to herself. She was much more of a "It's A Small World" kind of girl than a "Big Thunder Mountain Railroad" chick. But there was something about Space Mountain, something she wasn't quite sure she could articulate to Michael, not because it was all that difficult to explain, but because it sounded so silly when she explained it to herself.

Summer trips to Disney World had been something of a tradition for Michael's family. They'd gone four times that Veronica could remember, and they had the overstuffed photo albums to prove it. But for Veronica's family, the Disney experience had been a one-time thing. It was 1988, the summer before the Great Schism. Mom and Dad were doing their best impression of a happy couple, even carrying their act into the evening so that, after the first night, Veronica didn't bother to stay awake waiting for the sounds of their fighting to break through the thin hotel walls. Her brother Matt's performance wasn't so convincing, at least not to Veronica, who saw the glum expression that he wore at night, saw the ghost of that glumness in his face even when he smiled and played the part of the favorite son during the day.

Her most solid memory of that week—the rest of it was a blur of bright colors and the cheery sounds of children at play—was of the ride she and Matt took on Space Mountain, and of the aftermath of that ride.

She supposed now, with the power of hindsight at her command, that she should have known what was going on between the ride attendant and her brother as they snaked forward through the line. She remembered how odd it seemed to her that they kept staring at each other, but she also remembered writing it off as nothing more than boyish machismo.

"You nervous?" her brother had asked her once, or twice, or a half a dozen times. And now she realized, again through hindsight, that it had been as much a question for himself as it had been for her. As the attendant directed them to their car, there had been one last look shared between the two boys. And then Matt was back to his old sullen self. He made his way up front, and she sat behind him. They'd lost track of Mom and Dad, who'd probably been shunted off into a train on the other side.

It wasn't until they'd descended the slope, made their way through the tunnel of flashing blue light, and rocketed into the ride proper that Matt changed, changed for the moment and for good. As they rocketed through the darkness at thirty miles per hour, she heard a distinct change in his screams. They went from shrill yelps of terror to deep, guttural, almost primal bellows. He'd lost it. That's what she'd thought at the time. He'd flipped his lid. Matt screamed, "That the best you got?" as they hurtled down an unseen drop.

Veronica felt as if the very soul of her had lifted up out of her body for a moment, as they tumbled down, a heavy, leaden weight rising up out of her stomach and into her throat. And, for a moment, she was lost to the world. But then that weight came crashing back down into her, and she was back in that car, with her screaming sibling in front of her, and, try as she might to scream, she couldn't make a sound.

When they found Mom and Dad again, out in the center of Tomorrowland, Matt, breathless, told the lot of them that he was going back, that he wanted to ride it again.

It wouldn't be until later that night that Veronica would get the truth out of him. There had been no second ride. Instead, there had been a stolen kiss in a Tomorrowland bathroom, and a promise to meet up again before the week was over. Matt came back to the hotel room that night and confessed to Veronica who he was. "I like guys," he'd said. "And there's no use denying it anymore."

"Does this have anything to do with all that screaming you did on Space Mount—"

"Yes," he'd said. "A hundred times, yes. I mean, how many different ways could that ride have gone wrong, Veronica. And if you and I had died in there—"

"Died? Who dies on a roller coaster?"

"—if we had died in there, Veronica, think of how much in life you would have missed out on. And all because you were afraid, or because you were playing by someone else's rules about what you were allowed to do as a teenager, or as a girl, or as a boy who liked boys."

"You're a weirdo," she'd said. But the truth was that, even

back then, she'd thought he might be right. There had always been so much to be afraid of in their family. Fear seemed to be the motivating factor in every decision their parents made. And she wasn't sure she wanted to live like that. She wanted to be rid of fear in the same way that he appeared to be. Or, well, if not in exactly the same half-crazed way, then in some way, in some other way.

And yet, here she was, twelve years later, still quivering.

From behind her, Michael said, "So, it's that Space Mountain fills you with a Zen-like sense of peace, is that it?"

"I was just thinking," she told him. "Did you know that the summer before Matt came out to the family, he came out to me?"

"I always figured that you knew before the rest of us," said Michael.

"It was after we rode Space Mountain," said Veronica.

"Well, listen," said Michael, "I hate to break it to you, but I kinda figured out the truth about you and Desiree a long time ago. You know, even if you've never come right out and said it, a straight girl can only go to so many Ani shows before she's a gay girl."

Veronica smirked back at him.

"So, you're hoping what?" said Michael. "That you'll somehow find the courage to run away with Des just as soon as we're done here? That she and you will take Tracy and go hide away in some lesbian coven in Idaho or some damned place?"

"I'm not sure Idaho is the first place a group of gay girls would think of to hide out."

"Why not? All those potatoes..."

"Potatoes?" said Veronica, not following.

"All natural, easy to carve, come in all different sizes..."

Veronica laughed. "Cuz, you've got problems."

"Hey," he said. "apparently, it runs in the family."

She sighed. "I have the divorce papers in my purse, Michael. Or, well, Desiree has them, because she's got my purse. And I kind of figured that if I was ever going to find the courage to sign on the dotted line, it might be here. Right here, after this ride."

"Oh," said Michael. "Well then, I'm gonna get out and push, because there is no way I'm letting them give you enough time to change your mind about this."

Veronica reached a hand back toward him, as far as it would go.

"Are you trying to hit me?" asked Michael.

"Grab my hand, idiot," she said, and he did.

She squeezed his hand and said to him, "It's going to be hard for Tracy, without a dad around."

"The Runt was never much of a father to begin with," he said.

"Do you think," said Veronica, "that you...?"

"What about Matt?" said Michael.

"He's got his own issues to deal with," she said.

"Father figures are overrated," said Michael. "Two women, you guys'll do it much better."

"But," said Veronica. "If she needs someone."

Michael squeezed her hand back, but didn't say a word.

The overhead lights went off with a quick flash.

"Oh boy," said Michael. "Here we go."

"You know what to do, right?" said Veronica.

"No," said Michael. "What?"

"When this thing gets going, you've got to scream. You've got to scream your damned lungs out."

"Ah," he said, sounding unconvinced, "the people who scream on these things—"

"Don't be judgmental, Michael. Give it a try. Scream like there's no tomorrow. Scream like you have nothing to lose. And then just scream because you feel like screaming."

"Okay," said Michael.

"Ready?" said Veronica, pulling her hand back. The tunnel of blue light began to pulse again.

"Sure," said Michael.

"Hands in the air?"

"Okay," he said.

The train slipped forward, down the hill. Light and sound pulsed around them. And then, as they rocketed forward into the darkness, they began to scream.

And it felt good.

8

Veronica stood on a pedestal, chewing on a piece of bubblegum that had long ago lost its flavor. She watched the storefront window shudder in the November gale that raged outside and she sighed, wishing with all of her heart for just a moment of that breeze. Sweat dripped down along her bare back and down between her breasts. A spaghetti strap was sliding down her slick shoulder. On the couch in front of her sat two girls she hardly knew and the daughter who was becoming more of a stranger to her every day, each of them sweating as well, sleeves rolled up, sweaters discarded. And at her feet crouched a bony old seamstress, shivering in a shawl, fretting with the hemline of a dress that refused to fit, mumbling some kind of curse in some kind of old world tongue, the only kind of profanity which carried any weight anymore. Veronica gritted her teeth and swallowed her gum. It was going to be a while yet.

She was twenty-five years old, a tall shapeless mother-of-one in a slinky lilac gown that wasn't doing her worn-out body any favors. The same dress which had looked good on Mellie, the pleasingly plump sister of the bride, the same dress which the seamstress assured them, based on the measurements provided by email, would look stunning on Veronica's cousin Ashley, this dress seemed to want nothing to do with Veronica. A child-sized version of the ensemble even managed to make Tracy, Veronica's bookish tomboy of a daughter, look like some sort of princess, the heiress to the throne of the Purple Kingdom. But on Veronica, the dress just did not work. It hung on her like an undersized drape thrown carelessly over a coat stand. She had no hips to fill it out, and barely enough chest to hold it up. And yet, Tracy and Mellie would not cease showering her with compliments. "You look wonderful," said Mellie. "The most beautiful mom I know," said Tracy. Only Jenna, the bride-to-be, remained undecided.

"Jenna," said Mellie, "don't you think she looks good?"

Jenna frowned. "It's just not flattering on her, is it?"

Veronica could have kissed this girl, so relieved was she to finally have an ally.

The seamstress rose to her full height, her creaking joints crackling and popping as she did. She stepped backwards, away from Veronica, and sat on the arm of the couch.

"Do you see what I'm saying?" asked Jenna.

The seamstress chewed on the end of a pin. "I am not one to admit failure," she said.

"Oh," said Jenna, taking the seamstress's hand in her own, "that's not what I'm saying."

"But if ever I was to admit that my magic has left me," the seamstress continued, trailing off into a mumble.

Mellie frowned. "I still say she looks good," she said. Beside her, Tracy gave an exasperated sigh. The little girl picked up Veronica's pocket book, and began to rifle through it.

"What are you looking for, Trace?" Veronica asked.

"Nothing," said Tracy, continuing to dig. "Didn't you bring the Game Boy?"

"Auntie Ashley's old thing?"

"Yeah," said Tracy. "I was gonna play Tetris."

"We're almost done," said Jenna, smiling a weak smile at Tracy. "I promise."

Tracy pulled an envelope from the pocket book. "What's this?" she said.

"Put that back, please," said Veronica.

Tracy squinted, examining the return address. "This is from daddy's lawyer, isn't it?"

Veronica stepped down from the pedestal, and snatched the envelope away from her daughter.

"So," said Tracy, her face clenched into a frown. "That's it then."

"We've talked to you about this," said Veronica.

"You ruin everything," said Tracy, as she ran for the door, as she stormed out into the tempest.

❧

HAIL FELL FROM THE SKY, each stone ripping into the gooseflesh of Veronica's arms like a spitball sent from the mouth of Heaven. She stomped through the muck on the side of the road, calling out her daughter's name, imagining the worst. Cars blazed by, hydroplaning here and there, kicking up a spray of cold, dirty water as they passed. Veronica stumbled in their wake, caught herself, and then continued on. Tracy would not have been so lucky. She was too small, too frail. In her mind's eye, Veronica saw a tiny body flying up over the hood of an SUV.

"Tracy!" cried Veronica, picking up the pace. "TRAY-CEEEEEE!!!"

She shook her head to try and get the image out, tried to imagine Jenna and Tracy sitting at the snack bar of the Roller Kingdom again, the two of them splitting a plate of fries. It was an image that Mellie had painted for her while they worked to free Veronica from the shackles of her gown. And it was an image that made sense, she had to admit. It was right down the road, and Tracy did love it there, and, you know, why wasn't it possible that Jenna had found her before tragedy struck? Jenna had begun her pursuit before Veronica could even ask her for the favor. They were safe. That's all there was to it. And yet, Veronica couldn't help but sigh as she raced down the hill and toward the roller rink. She couldn't help but pause a moment before she opened up the door. Even if Tracy was alive, damage had still been done. The rift between them seemed more like a chasm now than ever before: deep, jagged, unbridgeable. Like the gash her brother had torn in the fabric of their family all those years ago, Veronica's attempt to be true had brought about a great schism of its own.

She opened the door and stepped backwards in time, back into the place that she herself had fled to so often, so long ago. The hall was dark and cavernous, the rink itself a halo of neon light at the center of the windowless purgatory. There were a dozen patrons, or thereabouts, and most of them were crowded around the outdated arcade games, the dusty old snack bar. Just like old times, there were only a handful of people on skates, and two of them, it turned out, were the two that Veronica was looking for. She leaned against the side of an out-of-order Pac-Man machine and watched them from the shadows.

Tracy whipped around the track as if trying to outrun the truth, or, as if, like Superman flying round and round the planet, she might be able to turn back time if she skated fast enough, hard enough. Veronica watched her daughter, and saw herself. In Tracy's eyes, there was such determination, such stubbornness, and such frustration. Tracy knew that this wasn't going to do any good, but she was going to do it anyway.

Jenna rolled off of the rink, and into the shadows. She came to a stop and bent over, hands on her knees, panting.

Veronica sighed. "She hasn't stopped since she got the skates on, huh?"

Jenna shook her head.

Veronica took a look at the skates. "We're the same size, right?"

Jenna nodded, rolling toward the nearest bench.

"She'll get over it," said Jenna, as she handed over the skates. "I know I did."

"How old were you?"

"Five, when my dad left. It was sad, but once I realized that there wasn't going to be any more yelling..." Jenna trailed off, managed a weak grin.

Veronica smiled, lacing the skates onto her own feet.

Jenna laughed. "Of course, with my mom's lousy taste in men, I've been through it three times now. So maybe I'm not the best person to ask."

Veronica stood, arms held wide at her sides, trying to keep herself upright. Tracy whipped by, a scowl on her face.

"Did you hate your mom?" asked Veronica.

Jenna sat silent for a second, and then she sighed heavy and hard. "I hated myself," she said.

That was worse, Veronica decided, so much worse. As she made her way out onto the rink, she couldn't shake Jenna's words from her mind. What if she, Veronica, had already done that kind of damage to Tracy? That would be unforgivable for certain, and maybe even unfixable to boot, and she didn't think she could live with herself if it were true.

Her little firecracker whipped up next to her, fuse burnt down almost to nothing. There was a little explosion in Tracy's high voice as she said, "How come you can't skate? Didn't you, like, live here when you were a kid?"

"I came on metal night," said Veronica. "Nobody ever skated. We sat in the booths, argued about the black album, head-banged to 'Bohemian Rhapsody'."

"Who's we?" asked Tracy. "You and daddy?"

"This was before I met him."

Tracy huffed and skated away. Veronica lowered her arms and

stumbled forward. Before I met him—those were the magic words, and Veronica couldn't believe she'd been stupid enough to utter them. "Tracy!" she shouted, pushing forward hard, tripping, falling onto her face. It took her breath away, the impact of her body hitting the floor, the sight of her daughter continuing on as if nothing had happened.

They were in the backseat of Jenna's beat-up Chevette before Tracy uttered another sound, and, once again, it was nothing more than an exasperated sigh. Up front, Jenna and Mellie stayed quiet. And though she knew that now was neither the time nor the place, she couldn't help herself.

"What do you want me to say?" she said.

"I want you to explain something to me," said Tracy.

Veronica glanced over at her daughter, surprised at how much venom an eight-year-old could muster, wondering if she herself had ever sounded so mean when she was so young.

Tracy frowned, gulped something down, and then spoke. "If you and daddy were a mistake, then what does that make me?"

Veronica reached for Tracy's hand, but the little girl pulled it away.

"That's what I thought," said Tracy, turning away.

Veronica felt her eyelids grow heavy and hot. How could she make her see? How could she get her to understand?

WHEN THEY GOT HOME, the Runt wasn't the only thing that was missing. Their apartment was empty, barren. All that was left was Tracy's bed, a single down comforter, and three boxes labeled 'Veronica's shit.' Tracy didn't say a word. She didn't throw Veronica so much as one nasty look. The little girl simply went to her room, sat on her bare mattress, and stared at the place on her wall where a poster of Sarah McLachlan had once hung.

Veronica read the note he'd left on the refrigerator without really reading it. She picked up her cell phone, ordered Chinese, and went back to her daughter's room to see how the kid was doing.

Tracy had opened one of the boxes. A photo album lay open on her lap.

"He brought most of your stuff to his new place."

Tracy nodded, flipped another page.

"He says the landlord expects us out by the end of the week."

Tracy looked up, her eyes a little swollen, a little red. "Where are we going to go?"

Veronica sat on the floor, leaned back against the wall. "Down the Cape, I think. The family's old summer house. Your grandfather will say no, but I think my Uncle Albert will overrule him."

Tracy gave her a little smile, then cast her gaze downward, her hand running over a crinkly page of the old photo album, smoothing it out.

"I'm sorry," said Veronica.

Tracy shrugged. "Whatever."

The doorbell rang and Veronica leapt up to answer it. By the time she returned with the enormous brown paper bag, Tracy had set the photo album aside and was examining a single snapshot. Veronica set their food down and sat down next to Tracy on the bed. She looked at the photo, a photo of Veronica and Desiree in their high school graduation gowns. Vern and Des were all smiles in the photo, the only evidence of their turmoil the glistening diamond on Veronica's ring-finger and the pregnant belly beginning to make itself known.

"Is it true that you're in love with someone else?" asked Tracy.

"What?" said Veronica.

"Daddy says that the reason you two don't get along is because you're in love with someone else. Is that true?"

Veronica bit down on her lower lip. She sat still and silent for a moment, but then, finally, she nodded her head.

"For how long?" asked Tracy.

"A long time," said Veronica.

Tracy ran a thumb over the photograph, left it hanging above Desiree's face. "Why didn't you marry that person then, instead of Daddy?"

"Because I'm a coward," said Veronica. And for a second, she thought of taking it back, she thought of revising her answer. But instead, because she knew it was true, and because she felt a weight lifting from her shoulders just by being honest, she said it again. "Because I'm a coward."

Tracy tossed the picture back into the open box, then slid to the floor. "Let's eat," she said. "Before it gets cold."

9

Veronica crouched at the foot of the Christmas tree, reaching under its lowest branches for the red metal stand that held the dying fir upright. Pine needles hailed down on her bare arm as she fumbled around for the first screw, her hand scraping against the trunk and slipping into the stand's soupy reservoir before she finally found it. She turned her face away from the shaking tree, squeezing her eyelids closed and biting softly on her extended tongue, and then, finally, she began to turn the screw.

Her father's heavy boots clunked along the living room floor. She felt the tree steady when the clunking came to a halt just to her left. And then, she heard his voice admonishing her. "You can't do that alone," he said. "The tree's going to fall on top of you. You'll get yourself killed."

"I was just getting it started."

"And besides," he said. "You're a guest here now. It's not your responsibility to clean up after your old man anymore."

Veronica sighed. She moved to the next screw.

"How is Tim?"

"I wouldn't know."

Robert grunted. "You can't even speak to the father of your child?" His voice trailed off. Then he grunted again. "What about when you drop Tracy off with him on the weekends? Like yesterday. Did you talk when you dropped her off then?"

Veronica shuffled herself around to the other side of the tree to work on the final screw.

"You don't even talk then?"

"We talk," she said. "But it's not exactly what you'd call a conversation."

Robert sighed. "Where did I go wrong in raising my kids? I mean, the two of you, you just... you seem determined to fuck up every good thing that's thrown at you."

"Done," said Veronica, ignoring him. "You can pull it out now."

"Oh," he said. "Okay. You just hold the stand then."

Robert groaned as he hoisted the tree out of the stand, and Veronica could hear him panting as he leaned it up against the wall.

"You want help carrying it out?" she asked him.

He looked up at her, then back down at the floor, and then he nodded.

They set the tree down on the curb, in front of his three overflowing garbage barrels, and beside the heap of flattened boxes they'd stuffed into his blue recycling bin. Robert put his arm around her, the first time he'd done that in years. And Veronica didn't like it. His glove, sticky with pine sap, clung to the shoulder of her pea coat. "I'm glad you came," he said. "I do wish you'd brought Tim, but—"

Veronica groaned. "I'm divorcing him, Dad. Please just get over it."

Her father wrenched his arm away from her and tended to a barrel in danger of tipping. "I like Tim," he said. "He makes an honest living. And he dotes on Tracy like any good father should."

"He's not her father," she said. "Michael is closer to a father than the Runt has ever—"

Robert stalked back toward the house. "I hate it when you call him that," he said. "He is your husband and the father of your—"

"He's neither!" she said, trudging after him through the snow. "Not anymore."

"And Michael? He's your cousin, not your... not a... and..." Robert trailed off, stopped to center himself, then found his heading again. "Michael is too young to be a father figure. And, besides, he's getting married, starting a family of his own with..." He trailed off again, his brow furrowing as he searched for her name. "That girl from Maine," he said.

"Jenna."

"Jenna," said Robert. "Sure. So, you can't count on Michael. And Veronica, you don't need to," he said, taking hold of her shoulders.

"Let go," she told him, trying to shrug him off.

"You've got Tim," he said as he let go of her, catching her drift a little later than she'd have liked. "You tell me: what's wrong with Tim."

"I'm not in love with him, Dad."

He stomped off again, reached down into the high snowbank as he passed it, balled up a clump of the stuff, and hurled it at the garage.

Veronica rolled her eyes and hurried after him.

The roar of the vacuum cleaner greeted her as she came in from the cold. Her mother was in her purple bathrobe, maneuvering the old Dirt Devil around the fireplace, getting it into every corner and crevice. The bathrobe was a plush, furry thing that hadn't fit her in five years. Lydia's body, which had never been what one would call trim or fit, at least not in Veronica's lifetime, had not withered, as Robert's had, as much as it had expanded. Like the overfull bag of the vacuum cleaner that she handled so deftly, it truly seemed as if she were about to burst.

From the kitchen came Robert's voice. "Coffee?" he shouted.

"You should buy her a new bathrobe," Veronica told her father. She took a steaming mug from him. "I mean, if you guys are going to pretend to play house again, why not go the whole nine?"

"You know, when I was running around the damned mall doing the Christmas shopping, I couldn't think of a damned thing. Not a damned thing." He sipped from his own mug and peered around the corner. "How could I have forgotten that she needed a new bathrobe?"

Veronica sipped at her coffee, but pushed it away almost as soon as it had touched her lips. One tiny slurp had been enough to scald the tip of her tongue, and it was bitter besides. "Dad," she asked, setting it down, "could I get some cream and sugar?"

"Did I forget?" he asked, picking up her mug for examination. "Christ, I'm sorry about that."

"It's okay."

He set down her mug on the countertop and opened the refrigerator. "Lot on my mind, I guess. You know how that goes, right?"

"I sure do," she said. "That said, I'm wondering if you've been to the doctor lately."

He scoffed. "I'm not losing my marbles, Veronica." He pinched open the top of the carton of cream and began to pour. "Tell me when," he said.

She held up her hand when he'd poured enough. In the living room, the vacuum stopped.

"Vern?" Lydia called. "Robert?"

"In the kitchen, Mum," Veronica shouted.

Lydia waddled in, smile on her face. She was much bigger since she'd quit the cigarettes, and Veronica saw that her father found it an effort not to frown. Closing the door on one bad habit, Robert had confided in Veronica, had just opened the doors to others. Lydia bought a donut with her morning coffee now, and at dinnertime she always made room for dessert. The holidays had been one night after another of pie and cookies and giggled "just one more"s. But what her father saw as folly, Veronica saw as good fortune. She remembered all too well the emphysemic hacking and wheezing of her grandfather near the end, and Veronica would much rather he had made the same trade her mother just had. After all, it was hard to hug a tombstone.

"Coffee?" Robert asked, holding up the pot.

Lydia waved a hand at him. "No, no, no. It's my New Year's resolution to start losing some of this weight," she said, rubbing at her belly. "I've put my mind to it."

She reached into the cavernous refrigerator and produced a gallon jug of spring water. Then she took her coffee mug—World's Best Grandma—down from the rack that hung above the stove, and she filled it to the brim.

Lydia came to the table, and sat beside her ex-husband, an exiled queen taking the throne beside her once and, perhaps, future king. And together, the two of them looked at their daughter, the princess who refused to play out the fairy tale ending they'd written for her, and they began to speak in unison, like some kind of Greek chorus trying to narrate for her how it was going to be. But before they could get a word out, Veronica backed away, dropping her mug into the sink, looking for an exit.

"I'm not going to listen to it," she said. "I should have known," she said. "I should have fucking known."

"Veronica," said Lydia. "All we're asking you to do is think of your daughter.'

"Think of Tracy," said Robert.

"I am thinking of Tracy!" shouted Veronica. "What you want me to do is repeat your mistakes, instead of learn from them."

"You think it was a mistake for me to stay with your father until you kids were grown up?"

"That wasn't a mistake," said Robert. "That's the way things should be done."

Veronica growled.

"Who's going to pay the legal fees?" Robert asked calmly.

"What?" said Veronica.

"Tim knows about you and..." He trailed off, seemingly incapable of saying Desiree's name. "Tim has evidence of adultery, Veronica. He'll bring that to court. He'll use it to win custody."

"He doesn't love her," said Veronica. "He doesn't want her."

"He does love her!" shouted Robert. And then, after a breath, he said, in a more measured tone, "And even if he doesn't, he'll take her just to spite you."

"To spite me?" said Veronica. "And that's the kind of man—"

"That's the kind of man you'll turn him into," said Lydia. "Believe me, Veronica. I know what the scorn of a woman can do to a man." She squeezed Robert's hand. "You're going to break the poor boy to pieces. He does love you."

"But I don't love him!" said Veronica. "I've said it again and again."

"Then who do you love?" asked Robert.

"I don't..." stuttered Veronica. "You know you don't want me to say her—"

"That's not allowed!" he shouted as he stood, knocking over his stool. "You can't... You..." His face was turning red as he struggled to find the words. "Not the both of you," he said. "Your brother, I can't do anything about him anymore. But you... No, not the both of you."

"I'll find the money myself," said Veronica. "If the Runt wants to make this a war, then Desiree and I will—"

"Stop!" he said.

"Stop what?"

"Don't say her name in front of me," said Robert.

"Robert," said Lydia, wrapping her hands around one of his forearms. "You should calm down."

"I'm bringing her to Michael's wedding," said Veronica. "She and I are—"

"You and her are nothing!" he screamed. "And you'll never be anything. This world won't let you be. And I—"

"This world, Dad? It's the year 2000."

"I won't let you be!" he shouted. "I want better for you, Veronica. I demand better of you."

"Can't you just accept—"

"The day I accept that is the day that I…" He trailed off. "You won't just be breaking Tim's heart," he said. "You'll be breaking mine, too."

"That's not fair," said Veronica. "That's not what I want to—"

"Love is never fair, Veronica. You should know that by now."

And with that, he walked away, sliding open the glass door behind him and stepping out onto the deck. Lydia, still in her bathrobe, still in her bare feet, stepped outside to join him.

Veronica watched her mother wrap an arm around her father's waist. She watched him return the favor. And then she felt sick to her stomach.

"The house," she said finally, because that was the whole reason for the visit, for the show she'd tried to put on. The performance she'd obviously bombed. "The house down the Cape," she repeated, clarifying.

"You moved in a month ago," he said, still not looking at her.

"Uncle Albert gave us the key," she said. "And yes, we've been living there. But I guess, I guess I wanted your blessing."

He grunted, then said, "What am I supposed to say?"

She stared at his back and imagined he was the Salesman instead, the version of him that she'd dreamed up a year ago. The Salesman might not have given her a blessing, but he would've found some roundabout way to let her know that he at least wasn't saying no.

"Are you going to try and kick us out?" she asked him. "I guess that's what I want to know."

"It's a long drive," he said, but did he mean that it was too long for him to drive to evict them? Or did he simply mean that she had a long drive ahead of her, and that it was time for her to go?

Veronica didn't ask. She turned and headed for her room, itching to pack, dying to get out of there.

10

There were five naked blondes on his living room floor, all of them clustered around a solitary brunette, fully clothed, with a missing tooth.

"Hey Tracy," said Veronica, as she stepped into her ex-husband's apartment, "why are they all—"

"Slumber party," said Tracy, cutting her mother off.

"A naked slumber party?" asked Veronica.

"Why not?" said Tracy. "You and Desiree have been having naked slumber parties for years. At least that's what Daddy says."

Veronica looked over her shoulder, back at Desiree, who was still standing in the hall. Des shrugged. Vern gave her a frown.

"You almost ready to go?" asked Veronica.

Tracy nodded, reached for her backpack, and then began to pack the dolls away.

As Veronica moved to collect Tracy's dirty clothes from the arm of the couch, her sleeping bag from the floor, and her books from the coffee table, she looked around for signs of her ex. "Where is he?" Veronica asked.

"Hiding," said Tracy.

From the doorway, Desiree asked, "He get you anything cool for Christmas?"

"Yeah," said Tracy. "A new doll. A really big one."

"How big is big?" asked Veronica. "We don't have a lot of room in the car."

"Oh, she's not coming with us," said Tracy. "She was a present for both me and Daddy."

"You're sharing a doll with him?" asked Desiree.

Tracy nodded. zipped up her backpack, and slung it over her shoulder. "I'm ready to go," she said.

Veronica looked at Desiree. Desiree arched an eyebrow as she looked back.

"Do you mind," said Veronica, "if we see the doll before we go?"

Tracy shrugged. "Sure," she said. "She's in my old room."

Veronica and Desiree followed Tracy down the hallway, whispering to each other as they went.

"Why is it her 'old' room now?" asked Desiree. "Why was she sleeping on the living room floor?"

"Why do you think?" said Veronica. "The Runt doesn't want her here. He never did. He only moved her things here in the first place to inconvenience me."

In front of them, Tracy pushed the bedroom door open, then stepped aside to let them in.

When Veronica saw what was inside, she had no words.

Desiree had three: "What the hell?"

"Isn't she pretty?" said Tracy.

The doll was not just big; it was life-size. It reclined on the bed that had once been Tracy's, head resting against the wall, a cowboy hat angled down over its face. It was a blonde, the doll, just like Tracy's toys. But, mercifully, it was not nude. It wore cowboy boots, a denim mini-skirt and a light blue tank-top pulled taut over a pair of enormous tits. Its skin was smooth and tanned and—Veronica couldn't resist—soft to the touch.

E. CHRISTOPHER CLARK

Desiree had knelt down beside the bed, was holding one of the doll's hands in her own. "It has a French manicure, Vern. I mean, a real French manicure. These look like real..." She trailed off, stared at the thing's chest. "And look at those things!" she said.

Veronica stepped around Desiree, toward the thing's head. She lifted the brim of the hat up, gasped, and took a step back.

"Ow!" yelped Desiree. "You stepped on my—"

"Did you see her face?" asked Veronica

"It," said Desiree. "It's an it, not a her."

"Can you take Tracy outside?" asked Veronica.

"Absolutely," said Desiree. "This is creeping me the hell out."

"What's so creepy about her?" said Tracy, as they disappeared down the hall.

Veronica peeked out after them, made sure they were gone, then lifted the hat off of the doll's face once more.

It was so real, so eerily real, except for that docile face. That was the sort of look that only happened in fantasies, the sort of look that said, 'Do with me what you will.' Veronica shuddered to think of what the Runt had done.

She ran her hand over the doll's blushed cheeks, through her blonde hair, across her pink lips. Then she stopped. She pushed gently on the lower lip, just to see, and the doll's jaw moved; her mouth opened. Veronica slid a finger over the tongue. It was wet.

"Christ," said Veronica.

She looked back at the door, then at the doll.

"Fuck it," she said, closing the door.

She kneeled down at the side of the bed and pushed the skirt up the doll's hips, revealing a pair of plain cotton panties to match the tank top. Then she pulled them to one side and found herself gasping again. There was a small triangle of pubic hair and beneath it a pair of perfectly sculpted labia.

"No way," she said to herself as she ran her fingers over them.

"No way," she said again as she parted them. "Oh my God," she said as she slid two fingers inside.

Behind her, the door opened.

"I assure you," said her ex-husband. "She's not your type."

Veronica stood and shook a slick finger at him. "This is nuts."

"Which part? The part where I've replaced you with 'the world's finest love doll' or the part where your daughter had a tea party with her this morning."

Veronica plowed past him into the hall.

"Yeah, go ahead and run away," he said. "Don't finish it."

"Finish what?" she asked, searching the living room to make sure that Tracy had not forgotten anything.

"This," he said.

"It is finished," she said. "We're finished."

"Oh no, we're not. There's still one thing left you have to say to me. And if you've never had an excuse before now, now you do."

"What, Tim? What am I supposed to say?"

The Runt laughed. "Tell me I'm not allowed to see her anymore."

"I don't get to decide that," said Veronica, heading for the door. "The judge—"

"Fuck the judge!" he said, getting in her way. "You know what the judge will say when you bring this to him, when you tell him I let our daughter play house with a sex doll. You know what he's going to say. So, say it yourself. Stop letting other people do the talking for you."

"Get out of my way," she said, balling up a fist, just in case.

"Say it," he said.

She swung at him, fist connecting with ear, and he went down, runt that he was.

"It's not just the judge's decision," she told him, as he lay prone, whimpering. "It's Tracy's. I can't make that decision for her. I won't."

She stepped over him and headed for the stairs.

❧

THAT NIGHT, in bed, Desiree turned to Veronica, shaking a book in her general direction, and asked, "Have you read this?"

Veronica gave the book's dust jacket a once-over, then nodded. "I grew up with an uncle who was obsessed with that band, then I lived in their old apartment for eight years. So, yeah, I've read it."

"Listen to this," said Desiree. "This is gross. And I quote, 'The album title worked on two levels. The first was the old biker ritual where a guy had to go down on his menstruating old lady before he could get his wings.'"

Veronica smiled. "It's pretty obscene, I'll give you that."

Desiree feigned a shiver, then closed the book. "I mean, how did they even prove it to the guys? Did they have to come out of the back room with a red mustache? And who was to say that they didn't use fake blood? Was there some sort of arbiter who checked the woman beforehand just to make sure?"

"I think you're overthinking this," said Veronica.

"All I'm saying," said Desiree, "is that you better not come near me when I've got mine."

"I know," said Veronica, with a chuckle. "Besides, we're all synced up now anyway. When I've got mine, I'm not even thinking about sex. Can't even stomach the thought of it."

"Good," said Desiree.

"You have to admit," said Veronica. "It's not nearly as gross as fucking a souped-up mannequin, though, is it?"

They chortled, collapsing against each other. Veronica pressed her face against Desiree's chest, felt her lover's laughter pound through her tired brain like a balm. She closed her eyes.

"Why didn't you tell him it was over, Veronica? That he wasn't allowed to see her anymore?"

"It's not my call," said Veronica.

"But he's dangerous, Vern. He shouldn't be around her."

"He's disgusting," said Veronica. "But he's not dangerous."

"He doesn't even want to be her father," said Desiree. "You said so yourself."

"But she wants him," said Veronica. "And as long as he's still Daddy to her, that's all that matters."

THEY WERE HEADED NORTH on Route 3 and driving past Plymouth when, from the back seat, Tracy asked, "Why didn't Desiree come with us today?"

"Well," said Veronica, "because we'll need the extra room for the ride home."

"For what?" asked Tracy.

"Your doll," said Veronica.

"You mean the big one?"

"Yep," said Veronica.

"But it's Daddy's, too."

"You don't think he'll let you borrow it?"

Tracy didn't answer. Veronica adjusted her rear-view mirror to get a look at the back seat.

"You think he won't share like he said he would?" asked Veronica.

"I think he likes the doll more than even I do," said Tracy. "Is that weird?"

"I don't know," said Veronica. "Do you think it's weird?"

Tracy was silent again. Then she said, "Maybe. Just a little."

"Well, I guess all you can do then is ask and cross your fingers."

"I hope he says yes," said Tracy. "Oh, and if he does, do you think Desiree would let me borrow one of her bikinis so I could take the doll to the beach?"

"It's January, sweetheart. Nobody's going to be at the beach."

"Oh, but the kids from the neighborhood, they'll see. And they'll come. And it'll be so cool. We'll all take pictures with her, us in our snow pants and her in the bikini!" Tracy began to laugh.

And because it was her daughter, and because that girl's laugh was as infectious as any plague the world had ever known, Veronica laughed with her.

BEFORE VERONICA LET Tracy out of the car, she made her promise to ask about the doll first thing.

"Will do," said Tracy. She pecked Veronica on the cheek and skipped up the steps of the apartment house. "See you in a couple of hours," said Tracy, waving over her shoulder.

"Bye!" called Veronica, checking the dashboard clock, then sighing. "Let's hope old habits really do die hard," she said to herself.

It took ten minutes for Tracy to come running back down the steps, her face pale except for her red eyes. She opened the front door and slipped into the shotgun seat, something she never did, even when Veronica gave her permission.

"Let's go," said Tracy.

"What happened?" asked Veronica, as Tracy slammed the door, as The Runt raced out of the building. He was shirtless, his hair disheveled, a pair of plaid boxer shorts all that covered him.

"He was on top of her," said Tracy. "And he was... He was moving up and down. And..."

The Runt stopped at the foot of the stairs and stared at Veronica. She watched his shoulders tense, his chest rise and fall. He clenched his fists. Come get us, Veronica dared him in her mind. Come and get us.

"I don't think he was expecting me, Mum. Was he expecting me?"

"I don't know what he was expecting," said Veronica. *But he got what he deserved*, she thought to herself. He got what he deserved.

"I don't want to see him anymore," said Tracy.

"Okay, sweetheart," said Veronica, buckling Tracy in. "If that's what you want."

11

That year it was Veronica's job to deliver the flowers to Grammy's grave. Everyone else was busy with preparations for her cousin's wedding and she was the one living in the Cape house anyway—the house that had been Grammy and Grampy's—so it just made sense. But her car was the worst, and there was a snowstorm on the way, so she couldn't wait for Desiree to arrive that evening with her everlasting Honda, and that was how Veronica and her daughter ended up broken down in the parking lot next to the Congregational Church, God's steeple casting a shadow over her as she took the Lord's name in vain.

"Mum," said Tracy. "Am I going to miss school? How am I going to hand out my valentines?"

Veronica laid her head down on the steering wheel.

"Do we have money for a tow truck?" said Tracy.

Veronica cast a glance over at the dozen red roses sitting on the passenger's seat. Then, she sighed. "Not anymore," she said.

"How about breakfast?" said Tracy.

Veronica sat up and searched for change. She dug between the car's seat cushions, plumbed the depths of the glove box, and fished around the cubby next to the cigarette lighter. "We've got enough for Dunk's," she said.

In his last months, her grandfather had made a request of the family that he called "simple": every Valentine's Day, place a dozen red roses on the grave of his late wife, their grandmother. It was a tradition he had begun early in their courtship, that he had continued on with after her death, and that he didn't want to imagine ending when he was gone.

"But isn't the snow just going to kill them?" said Tracy as they lay the flowers down.

"Yep," said Veronica.

In the coffee shop, they ate donuts and shared a hot chocolate. Tracy had a jelly and Veronica had a chocolate honey-dipped. There was a song on, coming over the shop's speakers, and Tracy sang along.

"How do you know the words to this?" said Veronica.

"I don't know," said Tracy.

Veronica frowned at her. "You don't think it's a little inappropriate?"

"Why?" said Tracy.

"Well, for one, your love doesn't cost a thing because it's not for sale yet."

Tracy sighed, kept singing.

"And for another," said Veronica, "do you have any idea what 'all the things' are 'that money can't buy'?"

"Love, Mum. Love. That's what The Beatles say, anyway."

Veronica smiled. "Well, I'm glad you've got taste some of the time."

They walked back past the car on their way home. Tracy's music player lay on the back seat. It had been a Christmas gift from the Runt, a costly piece of plastic about the size of a CD player that stored a hundred hours of digital music. Digital. What did that even mean? Veronica wondered, suddenly, how mixtapes would work with a thing like that. In seven or eight years, when boys were trying to woo Tracy, what would they do? Email her a bunch of files? What would they do for liner notes? Type them? Where was the romance in that?

"You want to bring your Nomad with us?" said Veronica.

"Oh my gosh," said Tracy. "I can't believe I forgot it."

The first flakes fell during their walk down Chatham Road, but it wasn't until they turned onto Deep Hole that things got miserable.

"Those poor flowers," said Tracy.

"I know," said Veronica.

"It's really romantic, though," said Tracy.

"Sure is," said Veronica.

"What's the most romantic thing you ever did for Desiree?"

Veronica smirked and snickered. Leaving the Runt when it made no financial sense to do so, she thought.

"What made no financial sense?" said Tracy.

"Did I just say that out loud?" said Veronica.

"You mumbled something," said Tracy.

"I guess I've never made a real, big, romantic gesture," said Veronica. "Got any suggestions?"

"You should write her a song," said Tracy. "A really good one."

At the piano that afternoon, in the cold dark of Grampy's living room—her living room now, she had to remind herself—Veronica played in circles, searching for the next chord. Each time she came round to it, the place where the bridge should have been, she found herself going back to the beginning. It grated on her, this timidness. She had never been this tentative with her guitar, and though it had been ages since she'd sat on this bench and plucked away at the old upright, since those summer days when Grampy would break out his trumpet to accompany her, she couldn't remember ever being so scared.

She slapped both hands down on the keyboard, her lead foot lowering the boom on the sustain, and she closed her eyes, letting herself be swallowed up by the wall of noise. She leaned her forehead against the rough wood, unpolished for almost a decade now, since before Grampy died. It was cool against her skin and it was only then, as she felt her flesh slip into the piano's ornamental grooves, that she noticed the sheen of sweat that had covered her. Down the hall, a door slammed open and the hall light flashed on. A pair of feet shuffled toward her.

"That was it!" said Tracy.

"That was it?" said Veronica. "That was garbage."

"Nuh-uh," said Tracy. "It was pretty, except for the end. Just needs words."

Veronica turned to face her daughter, straddling the bench as she did. "The words are the hardest part, Trace. There's a reason I only do cover songs."

"What about that one you sang to me when I was a baby?"

"That was one song," said Veronica. "One song out of ten years worth of trying."

Tracy gave a heavy sigh, shook her head, and stalked off toward her bedroom again. Once the door slammed shut, Veronica got back to it.

Desiree walked in ten minutes later.

"Hey," she said. "Why'd you stop playing?"

"I don't know," said Veronica.

"That was one of my favorites," said Desiree. "I haven't heard you play that in years."

Veronica lifted an eyebrow at her lover.

"What?" said Desiree. "That was the one you wrote for your brother's play, right? The one back in high school?"

"You've heard that song before?"

"Yes," said Desiree. "It was the song the troubadour sang to Sleeping Beauty to try and wake her up."

"After all the kisses had failed," said Veronica.

Desiree sat down beside her on the bench. "I loved that play so much," she said.

Veronica set her fingers back on the keyboard, trying to remember the rest of the song.

"I think most people were too dim to figure it out," said Desiree. "But not me. I got it. And when the princess woke up for that moment, just after the singer had admitted defeat and left. God, that got me every time."

"Every time?" said Veronica.

"Yeah," said Desiree. "I went every night the weekend it played."

Veronica ducked her head. Then she took Desiree's hand in her own and squeezed.

"What?" said Desiree. "What's wrong?"

"You don't have to work at it," said Veronica. "You don't have to work at loving me."

Desiree gave a brief laugh. "And you have to work at loving me?"

Veronica looked up. "That's not what I meant," she said. "It's just that... it's so hard sometimes to do the right thing, to say the right thing. And then I look around at people like you, like my grandfather—as hokey as it was, his roses, they were his thing, and he believed in them, and it worked."

Desiree worked her hand free of Veronica's, then placed Veronica's hands back into their positions on the piano. "Play me the song," she said.

Veronica shook her head. "I don't know it. I can't remember the bridge."

Desiree hummed the tune. She was off-key, but she got the point across.

"That was it?" said Veronica. "That's so damned obvious. How did I not—"

Desiree set two fingers to Veronica's lips. "Just play," she said.

"But the words," said Veronica.

"Make them up," said Desiree. "Those I can't remember."

So, Veronica played. She looked out the window, at the snow

falling faintly and faintly falling, wondering where those words were from, that turn of phrase. It wasn't hers, she knew, but she sang it anyway. Always cribbing from somewhere, always propping herself up with the work of someone else. She shook her head, and was about to stop. But then Desiree laid her head upon Vern's shoulder. And that was enough to keep her going.

12

At seventeen, somewhere between four and five months pregnant, as a great big fuck you to the rumor mill, Veronica closed out a talent show with a scorching guitar solo she played whilst standing atop her high school's grand piano. And her life as a musician had been pretty much downhill from there. A few months later, she married the sad sack—*the runt*—who knocked her up. Sure, her father paid for four years at Berklee in exchange for her "loyalty"—whether to the Runt or to her dad's heteronormative stance on love and marriage, she was never sure—but she'd never had enough time to really learn anything, despite how much she was taught.

"It was actually the middle school's piano," Veronica told her daughter as they loaded her gear into the auditorium.

"You mean that one up there?" Tracy asked, pointing at the stage.

"Yep," said Veronica, as they walked the aisle. "When they built the high school across the street in the seventies, they forgot to build an auditorium. Or else they were being cheap and figured they could just keep on using this one over here."

"So, wait," said Tracy, huffing, straining under the weight of a guitar case she shouldn't have tried to carry herself. "Did this building used to be the high school?"

"Yes," said Veronica, plucking the case from her daughter's hands. "Until 1974. My Uncle Albert was the last class to graduate here."

"So," said Tracy, collapsing into a seat in the front row, "the piano could still technically be the high school's, depending on how old it is."

"The piano's not that old," said Veronica, hoisting her stuff up onto the stage. "It would have to be older than me."

"Oh," said Tracy. "And that's pretty old."

Veronica did not correct her.

Up on stage, Vern's cousin Michael was giving instructions to the members of his old high school band. They were reuniting for what would be the penultimate event of Wedding Week: a concert on the same stage where they'd played their first gig many moons before. In her head, Veronica did the math. Tracy had been two and a half then, and Veronica's biggest accomplishment to that point in her career at Berklee was the venomous dirge she'd made of Ini Kamoze's "Here Comes the Hotstepper."

Veronica slumped into a seat beside her daughter.

"You know," said Tracy, "they're pretty awesome."

"You've heard them before?" asked Veronica.

Tracy dug around in her backpack and produced her Nomad, headphones coiled around it. "Yep," she said, patting her music player. "I have their demo tape and their seven inch."

Veronica turned to face her daughter. "And how, may I ask, did you come upon those? Napster?"

"No way," said Tracy. "Too dangerous over there now. I'm using Kazaa these days."

"So, you stole your uncle's music?"

Tracy groaned. "How could I steal it if it's not for sale anywhere? You're crazy sometimes."

Veronica mussed Tracy's hair. "It runs in the family," she said, as she watched her cousin descend from on high to mingle with the commoners.

"Hey," said Michael.

"Hey yourself," said Veronica.

"What you listening to?" asked Michael.

Veronica turned to look at Tracy, who had slipped her headphones on. "Tracy, take those off. That's rude."

"How's it rude?" said Tracy. "I'm listening to his band!"

"But we're about to play," said Michael, chuckling.

"Really?" said Tracy, pressing play on her Nomad. "Because it looks like you're about to talk."

❧

TRACY'S favorite song by Gideon's Bible, Uncle Michael's band, was the one they rehearsed first with Veronica. It was called "Mistake," and though she wouldn't know what it was really about until years later, when she wrote an explication of it in high school, she had a sense, even at eight years old. The growl of her uncle was what got that across, the palpable anger in every hiss and snarl. "He was a mistake," roared Uncle Michael, "she was a mistake," he continued, "and I was a," he screeched, trailing off as the guitars kicked in.

And oh, those guitars. Veronica's was solid, a foundation on which to build upon, but the other girl on guitar, she was fierce. Her name was Robin, and Tracy had heard she and Uncle Michael used to date. Tracy looked around the auditorium for Jenna, the girl Michael was going to marry, to see if she looked jealous. She didn't. She had a smile on her face, was nodding her head to the beat. Nope, she didn't look jealous at all. But she should have. Dancing was cool—that's what Jenna did; she danced—but to shred on a six-string, that was something else.

When the band broke for fifteen, Robin grabbed the seat beside Tracy and sat down. "I hear you're a fan," said Robin.

Tracy ducked her head, nodding. She was sure she would cry or faint or otherwise embarrass herself if she looked Robin in the eye. She had listened to little else besides Gideon's Bible since finding their stuff online a month before. Aside from "Mistake," the songs Robin sang were the ones she listened to the most.

On stage, Veronica sat at the piano and noodled away at the song she'd written for Desiree back on Valentine's Day. She looked at her fingers as she played, then looked up at the ceiling, but never out into the empty auditorium, never at any of the people lurking in the wings.

"Your mom has no idea how good she is," said Robin. "Does she?"

"She says you put her to shame," said Tracy, focusing her gaze on the screen of her Nomad, on the flashing battery indicator.

"Really?" said Robin, with a chuckle. "Before you showed up, I was telling the guys how jealous I was of her, how nervous I was to be playing next to the one and only Veronica Silver."

"Nervous?" said Tracy, finally looking at Robin. "You?"

"Oh yeah," said Robin. "The whole thing makes me nervous, really."

"Because you and Uncle Michael used to date?"

Robin looked at Tracy, gave her a smile. "That's part of it, sure."

"Hmm," said Tracy.

"Hmm?" said Robin.

"I'm trying to decide something," said Tracy.

"What's that?" said Robin.

"Who's the Desiree in this story? That's what. Is it you, or is it Jenna?"

Robin raised an eyebrow. "Is Desiree the good guy or the bad guy?"

Even after all these months, Tracy hadn't decided the answer to that question yet. So, she said, "Neither. She's the Desiree."

WHEN VERONICA LOOKED up from the piano, Tracy was in deep conversation with Robin. It was a strange sight, Robin sitting sideways in her chair, knees tucked up under her chin, listening intently to the story Tracy was telling her. Even in her street clothes—torn jeans, a red flannel, and an *Appetite for Destruction* tank top—she looked like a rock star. But sitting the way she sat, nodding along as she stared into the eyes of the little girl holding court before her, Robin also looked like she might just be a cool babysitter, the kind you hoped to get as a kid, but were scared to have hired as a parent.

"What do you suppose they're talking about?" Michael asked Veronica as he sidled up beside her.

"Surely, they're addressing the injustice of Janet Jackson topping the charts again," said Veronica.

"Good call," said Michael. "I was thinking they might be tackling the sociopolitical realities of electing a crackhead President of the United States."

Veronica laughed.

"You ever worry," said Michael, "about the world we're leaving behind for her?"

"I ain't leaving shit behind yet," said Veronica. "I'm not done with the world myself."

"You know what I mean," said Michael.

Veronica wrapped her arm around Michael's shoulders and gave him a squeeze. "I do," she said.

Out in the front row, Robin was waving them over. "Michael!" she shouted. "Veronica!" And then she turned, searching the seats for someone else. "Jenna!" she cried, waving her over, too.

They congregated around Tracy, who was biting her lip and tapping her sneakers against the seat, her knees tucked up under her chin now, just like Robin's.

"What's up?" asked Veronica.

Robin looked at Tracy and nodded to her, as if to say, go ahead. But Tracy said nothing.

"Trace," said Michael. "Did you want to tell us something?"

"She wanted to ask us something," said Robin.

Tracy shook her head in a silent no.

"Okay," said Robin, looking at Tracy, as if for approval. "You want me to say it?"

It took Tracy a moment, but she did nod.

"Okay," said Robin. "Tracy is wondering who the Desiree is in Michael's story: Jenna or me."

Veronica felt her jaw drooping. She looked over at Jenna, wanting to apologize, but not wanting to hurt her daughter's feelings by saying "I'm sorry" out loud. It was a valid question, she supposed, just phrased poorly, and perhaps not something Tracy should have asked one of the parties involved.

"Wow," said Michael, leaning back against the edge of the stage. "I'd never thought about my story having a Desiree in in it."

"Well," said Veronica, attempting to lighten the mood, "your story does have a Desiree in it, but that's a whole other chapter."

She looked around, waiting for a chuckle, but none came.

Jenna sat down in the seat one row behind Robin's and leaned toward Tracy. "You're worried Uncle Michael might be marrying the wrong girl?"

Tracy looked down, bit her lip harder. A tear rolled down her cheek as she nodded.

Michael crouched down in front of Tracy, lifted her chin up. "Honey," he said. "That is the sweetest..." he said, then trailed off, crying a little himself now. "But you needn't worry. Let me tell you a story."

He told the kid-friendly version of it, but Veronica knew this story, knew it well, so her mind filled in the blanks as he went.

MICHAEL'S FAMILY hadn't had to set the leaf into the middle of their dining room table in years, not since Grammy and Grampy were both still alive and still living upstairs, not since Veronica's family had moved from across the driveway to across the town. But that night, the night that Robin met Jenna, the night Jenna met everyone in fact, there were six of them. And though they had been cramming five around the unextended table for years—thanks, of course, to Robin—six just wasn't possible.

Jenna was, at that point, just a college housemate of Michael's, a friend crashing in the spare bedroom. Her work-study job had offered her extra hours over spring break, and it was an offer that she, like many a poor scholarship student, could not refuse. The dorms were closed, and commuting from her home in Maine certainly wasn't an option, so Michael had offered her a room. It was as simple as that. Or, well, it should have been. But things were never simple when his little sister got involved. Ashley loved drama, and she was constantly looking for ways to pull people's strings.

"It's lucky you live with Michael," was how it began. "He's never been able to say no to a pretty girl in his life."

"Ash!" said their father, as Jenna gave an uncomfortable chuckle, ducking her head and pushing a stray lock of her auburn hair behind her ear.

Robin went scarlet. And that was all it took for everything to unravel. Two girls who might have gone through the entire evening without so much as an indifferent glance toward one another were now adversaries. Ashley was excused from the table, her mother glaring after her.

"It's too bad you have to work through your break," said Robin. "That's so sad."

Jenna forced a smile. "I don't mind really. Spring break's never really been a time to party for me. My mother's never been able to afford that luxury."

Robin frowned and gave her a supercilious little nod. "Michael and I were supposed to join some friends in Cancun," she said. "He says he decided against it because he has a lot of painting to catch up on. But we both know what the truth is, don't we?"

Jenna shook her head. "I'm afraid not."

Robin smirked. "The truth is that Michael decided against it because he has no idea how to have a good time." Robin laughed, and then added, "At least, not like he used to."

Michael stayed quiet, as was his wont. Speaking up wasn't going to prove anything. And it might just make matters worse. The real truth of the matter was not that Michael didn't know how to have a good time. The truth of the matter was that Michael's idea of a good time and Robin's idea of a good time were two paths slowly diverging from one another in the increasingly frosty woods of their relationship. Booze and bongs and hot bods—those were Robin's turn-ons. There was always some new beer to try out with her, some new drug she'd gotten from a friend of a friend of a friend. And lately, there were the constant hints that another body crammed into bed might spice up their lackluster love life. But up at the college, away from Robin (she was in Boston, at Berklee), Michael had been discovering, or, rather, rediscovering, that those things weren't his cup of tea. He'd learned that a quiet afternoon at the pond, with a couple of issues of *X-Men* to read, was far more enjoyable for him than a hit of X at some kegger in some Boston dorm room, obnoxious drum-n-bass blaring in the background. He'd decided that the *Rent* sing-a-long parties at his townhouse were a lot more fun than the stressful gigs that Gideon's Bible had been putting on these past few months. And he knew, in his heart of hearts, that a girl like Jenna, a girl he could talk to, a girl who was as comfortable with silence as she was with a roaring stereo, was the kind of girl he should be with. He kissed Robin. He fucked Robin. He played hard-nosed, kick-ass rock and roll with Robin. But he couldn't remember the last time he'd had a conversation with her about something other than kissing, or fucking, or rock and roll.

That night, the fucking happened in the back row of theater number four at the old Route 3 Cinema across town, the dingiest, most filthy room in the place. Screwing at the cinema was something she had always wanted to try, and though they had fooled around back there before—French kissing, heavy petting, et cetera—they'd never gone all the way. To sate her, and to hopefully put an end, at least temporarily, to all her talk about threesomes, Michael had consented to give it a try. But he was still nervous about the whole thing. Yes, the construction of the new movie theater down the street had given the staff at Route 3 a kind of "Screw it. What's the point?" mentality when it came to rules enforcement, but fucking in the back of a movie theater was still fucking in the back of a movie theater, and Michael didn't like the idea of being caught, regardless of whether or not he was going to be punished for it.

She rode him while facing the screen, so the both of them could still watch the movie. And, as his sneakers stuck and then unstuck themselves to the floor, it occurred to him that the sticky residue there might not be entirely the fault of spilled soft drinks and discarded chewing gum. It was an unpleasant thought, but, thankfully, not one he had to focus on for long. From the time she hiked up her skirt and shimmied onto his lap until the time that she shimmied off and headed for the bathroom, no more than three minutes could have passed. The more risqué the situation, the quicker she was done. And, of course, that was part of the problem. They were running out of things to try. Doing something while driving: that was next. And maybe, he found himself thinking, they would crash and burn, and it would all be over, all of it.

While he was driving her home, Robin wound herself tight around his free arm, squeezing his hand between her thighs. She purred against him, warmer than she should have been on this cold night, in this cold car, with its busted heater. "What about

Jenna?" she asked, as they turned off of the main drag and onto her road.

"What about Jenna?" Michael asked, trying, gently, to extricate his hand from the prison of her legs.

"Well," said Robin. "You like her. That's obvious."

Michael shook his head and turned away from her.

"What?" said Robin, pulling herself off of him as they pulled up in front of her house. "Tell me you haven't imagined it."

Michael turned to face her again, rubbing the numbness from his freed hand. "I haven't imagined it, Robin. I don't imagine those kinds of things."

"Sure you do," she said, opening her door. "You just won't admit it."

"This is a fine way to say goodnight," he said.

And then, Robin stepped out of the car, and slammed the door behind her. And somewhere, deep inside, he knew that, finally, this was the beginning of the end.

There was a light on in the upstairs living room when he got home, and Michael felt his shoulders loosen up at the sight of it. Just as it did up at school, the warm glow of a second story window was all it took to set him at ease. Jenna was still up, and that meant that, for once during one of these horrible sojourns back home, he was going to have someone to vent to.

He let loose a heavy sigh once he'd reached the top of the stairs. Jenna looked up from the pages of *Dance Kinesiology* and gave him a smile. "That bad, huh?"

Michael plopped down onto the couch next to her. She set her book down on the floor and patted two hands on her lap. Sighing again, he laid back, resting his head on her legs. She ran her fingers through his hair, rubbed at his temples. "Spill it," she said.

"Why am I still with her, Jenna?"

Now it was Jenna who sighed. And then groaned.

"You said you wanted to hear it," said Michael.

"I think I changed my mind," she said. "A woman's prerogative, you know."

Michael chuckled.

"Okay," she said. "Go ahead."

He spilled the beans on the whole evening, up to and including Robin's latest proposal for a ménage à trois. And he felt no remorse for being so open, for sharing. Because this is what they did at the college. They were honest with one another, and they leaned on each other when they needed to. Like a family. That was what was at the heart of it. Kimball College and Jenna, most of all, had reminded him what a family was supposed to be like. Up there was not like down here, in "greater" Lowell, where the lies came as fast and furious as the Merrimack came over the Pawtucket Falls, where you were on your own from start to finish.

At the end of his story, Michael felt Jenna's taut belly ripple with laughter against the crown of his head.

"What's so funny?"

She collected herself, then said, "That she'd want to share you with me."

Michael gave her a smirk. "You think she wasn't serious?"

"Oh," said Jenna, "I'm sure she was serious. That girl feels like she's got something to prove. But, you believe me, Michael: if I ever got ahold of you, you'd never go back. I wouldn't let you go back, and you wouldn't want to."

Michael felt a rush of blood away from this face, away and down, toward a lower place. He hoped she wouldn't notice.

"You're a great guy, Michael, and your girlfriend's an idiot for not knowing that. She's always seen you as having the raw material to be a good man, as someone she would have to shape and mold, and she's thrived on that. But now that you're coming to the realization that you are a good man—no assembly required—she's getting desperate."

Michael frowned. "How desperate, do you think?"

Jenna was silent for a moment. And then she asked, "Are you sure you want my opinion on this?"

Michael nodded.

"It's only a matter of time before she finds someone, Michael. If you won't be shaped to her liking anymore, then she's going to go find someone who will. That's what girls like her, women like her... that's what they do." Jenna stopped rubbing his head. "That's why my mom's had kids with three different men, why she's been through two divorces and is working on her third."

Michael reached up, squeezed her hand.

"Most women I know, Michael... they want a man they can fix." She sighed again, looked down at him. "Even me, I guess."

Michael sat up, turned around to face her, grabbed her other hand. "Don't," he said. "You know that he's a good guy, deep down."

Jenna's gaze remained fixed on her lap. "How deep, though?"

They looked at each other and sighed.

"Some other time," said Michael, wistfully.

"Some other place," she said, finishing the familiar refrain of their friendship. And then she hugged him. She hugged him closer and longer than she ever had before.

They parted, she stood, and then she ruffled his hair. "It'll all work out in the wash, Michael."

He nodded, and smiled at her mixed cliché. "I guess so."

⚜

TRACY WAS CONFUSED. "So," she said, "you should be with Jenna because she likes kissing less than Robin does?"

Everyone looked at Michael, who was sitting on the floor now, each of the women giving him a puzzled smirk. It was like they were wondering how he was going to answer the question, too.

Michael stared at Tracy, a warm smile on his face, but she focused on his eyes, because the eyes were where the truth was; she'd read that somewhere. His were hazel, or so he'd told her when she asked him time and time again, and though she'd never known before what hazel meant, now she had an idea. His eyes were a greenish brown, but there were flecks of blue in there too, of gold. She was sure, if you stared deep enough into Uncle Michael's eyes, you could find any color you were looking for. But she wasn't sure whether that was good or bad, or what it meant about him and the truth.

"No," he said. "That's not it. What I'm trying to say is that, we meet a lot of lovely people in our lives, Tracy. Sometimes, it's the first person that we're meant to be with. And sometimes it's the last one. Does that make sense?"

"Kinda," she said. "But," she said, and then trailed off, thinking about something. There was this photograph of Robin and Michael, back in their high school days, singing into the same microphone, smiles cracking through the masks of their serious rock and roll faces, and Tracy, she had just seen them do the same thing up on stage. They had just looked at each other in the same way, like they loved each other, like they each knew that there was no one else in the world who could make them feel like they did in that moment.

"What about when you sing those songs to each other?" said Tracy. "The songs you wrote to each other in high school?"

"Well," said Michael, "you've heard those songs. We were angry at each other, most of the time."

Robin laughed. "That we were."

"Most of the time," said Tracy. "But not all of the time."

Jenna put a hand on Tracy's shoulder and Tracy thought to shrug it off, because she was still pretty sure Jenna was the bad guy here, and she didn't want her ears filled with Jenna's lies. But she stayed still, because there was something she wanted even less than that, and that was a scene. So, she let Jenna speak.

"Tracy," said Jenna, "you've seen the plays they put on in the barn down the Cape, right?"

Tracy nodded.

"When we sing to each other now," said Robin, "it's like that. We're pretending. We're playing the people we were years and years ago."

Veronica crouched down to say something to Tracy now. "And that's what I was doing with the... with your father, Tracy. Pretending. Putting on a show. If you want to know who the Desiree is in Uncle Michael's story..."

"I get it," said Tracy, standing up, tired of all their words and explanations, ready for the scene now, if it was going to come. "I just want to be alone for a while."

She picked up her Nomad and her headphones, then walked up the aisle and out of the auditorium. She cast a glance or two over her shoulder, to see if anyone was following her, but all she saw was Michael holding Veronica's hand as she stood, maybe to move, maybe to come after Tracy, before she sat down again and let Tracy go.

❧

VERONICA COULD HAVE PUNCHED her cousin right then, but maybe he had a point. Maybe the kid needed some space. The school was a safe enough place. She couldn't get into too much trouble there. And the band had a few more songs to run through anyway, the covers in particular, and "November Rain" chief among them.

Veronica was flabbergasted when Michael mentioned the song by name, the song she'd made her one fleeting mark with, but Robin was taken aback by Veronica's disbelief.

"That solo," said Robin, "that solo you did, it's legend. Better than Slash's."

"Now you're just being ridiculous," said Veronica, shooting her cousin a glance, to see if this were all for real.

"Veronica," said Michael, "we are not going to pass up this chance for you to relive your glory days."

"Glory *day* is more like it," said Veronica. "Singular. And really," she continued, "it's not the same without the orchestra."

"Which is why," said Robin, "we've invited them to join us this evening."

"Chelmsford's finest," said Michael.

Her cousin really was too much. This was supposed to be his moment, his last fling before settling down. That he'd taken the time to make this happen, to make this happen for her, that was... Veronica looked out into the audience, searching for Jenna, who was all smiles as usual. That was one lucky girl, Veronica thought.

Michael brought Veronica her guitar, the one she'd played on this stage, on that song, nearly nine years before. She didn't mess with it much these days, because of its wonky pick-ups, its tendency to fall out of tune after three minutes, and the high E's fondness for snapping mid-performance.

"This one's temperamental," she told him.

"But would you play it on any other axe?" said Robin.

Veronica shook her head in a silent no.

"Good," said Michael, as Veronica slung it over her shoulder. "Now, if you'll excuse me, I'm going to leave you two to sort out who plays which solo. I've got a little girl to cheer up."

"I thought you said she needed space," said Veronica, as Michael leapt off stage, then bounded up the aisle.

◈

WHEN MICHAEL FOUND HER, Tracy was sitting halfway up the lobby's grand staircase, the monstrosity that led to the second floor. Her Nomad was blaring "A Toast to the Duplicitous" through her headphones, and it was only when he sat down beside her that she noticed he was there.

She paused the song, asked him, "Whatever happened to David?"

"David?" said Michael.

"The other founder of Gideon's Bible," she said, clarifying.

Michael sighed. "Love triangle," he said, and when she just stared at him, waiting for more, he added, "It's a long story."

Tracy grunted. "That's the only kind of story grown-ups ever have," she said. "And they never tell them."

Tracy set her gaze on the the road just beyond the enormous two-story wall of windows that rose from the floor in front of her, that imposing tower of glass. Michael was rambling on about something that was supposed to make her feel better, but what she found herself thinking about were the friends she was making back home in Harwich—for that really was home now, she had to admit. She found herself thinking about which of the boys she would fall in love with, which of the girls would be her best friends, who she would betray first, and who would betray her.

"Tracy," said Michael, "I didn't mean to make you cry again."

"Why can't people just be nice to each other?" she said, wiping with her long sleeve at the tears she didn't realize she'd been crying.

"I don't know," said Michael. "And I realize that's a shitty answer, but..."

Tracy looked at him, wide-eyed. He didn't seem embarrassed at all about the word he'd just used. He was just staring off through the windows now, like she had, as if searching for his next thought. Tracy thought to admonish him for his potty mouth, the way she did Veronica and Desiree, but she didn't. Uncle Michael was supposed to be like her father now—she'd overheard her mother saying as much to Desiree—and he kind of was, the way that he tried to make her feel better, the way he felt the need to keep talking until she was distracted from her pain, or whatever she'd been complaining about. But he also kind of wasn't. He also kind of didn't have to be. She had two parents already, or three, depending on who you counted. Uncle Michael was free to be something else, free to be the guy who said "shitty" when that was the best word for the job.

"Are you going to break up with Jenna," said Tracy, "because of what I said?"

"What?"

She sniffled. "Because I didn't mean to do that," she said. "I just like it when you're happy, Uncle Michael."

He put his arm around her, lifted her up onto his lap. "And I like it when you're happy," he said, tickling her sides.

She giggled, then smiled.

Michael held her close. "Listen," he said. "I can't say for sure that Jenna and I will always be happy together. Your mom can't say for sure about Desiree, either. Once upon a time, we were all happy in different places, with different people. And who's to say that someday there won't be some other person, when we're in some other place?"

"But that's not fair," said Tracy. "That's not right."

"You're right," said Michael, "but we can't control the future, and we can't rewrite the past, no matter how much we'd love to. All we can do is enjoy the here and now."

"I guess," said Tracy. His answer wasn't good enough. No grown-up's answer ever was. But it would do, for now.

"So," he said, standing up and hoisting her up as he went, "you want to go see a concert?"

❧

Veronica had forgotten how boring the song was. At nearly nine minutes long, and minus the epic video starring the epically gorgeous Stephanie Seymour, there were long stretches of piano playing and oohing and ahhing from the backup singers where she felt herself stifling yawns. But, when the final guitar solo drew near, when the band stripped the opus down to its core, just the piano and the drums, when it was time for her to climb the steps that led to the top of the piano, she was ready.

She focused on the guitar as she began, drowning out everything but the music, which she let envelop her. But in the middle, in the middle it occurred to her that there was something more she wanted to see in this moment than her fingers bending the disobedient strings to her will. She was nervous to look out into the crowd, because splitting her focus, especially during a solo, had always seemed like hubris to her. But then, suddenly, she remembered her dream, remembered the message her younger self had tried to impart. Veronica looked down. She was standing on top of the piano. On top of it! She would have laughed, if laughing were allowed in a serious rock and roll moment like this. Instead, she turned her gaze to the front row, to the little girl who sat—no, stood!—there.

Tracy's mouth was agape when Veronica locked eyes with her, still not comprehending that this was her mother up there, wailing away. But then Veronica said something to her daughter with the guitar, something crazed and filled with passion, a plea: "Let go."

That was when Tracy began to headbang, along with everyone around her. People pointed, as if to say "Look at that bad-ass kid," then got back to their own raucous response, recharged by her exuberance.

Look at that bad-ass kid, thought Veronica. My kid.

Atop the piano, Veronica lost herself in the music, playing the shit out of her guitar—playing *the shit* out of it—until they all came crashing down together.

The Silver Family's story continues in The Boot of Destiny, *wherein Veronica's bad-ass kid puts her Uncle Michael on trial for his "crimes against femininity."*

ACKNOWLEDGEMENTS

A portion of this novel was originally performed as the stage play *A Lick and a Promise*. This play was presented as part of the Spring 1998 Student Theater Festival at Bradford College in Haverhill, Massachusetts.

The cast of that production included Robyn Blanchard as Veronica, Robert DaPonte as Tim (the Runt), Amanda Damstra as Tracy (not Veronica's daughter Tracy, but an early version of Desiree with a different name), and Chris Larsen as Andy the Chinese Food Delivery Boy. I directed, with assistance from my good friend Jim Arrington.

❀

Another portion of the novel was originally performed as the stage play *Crossroads (or The Piano of Death)* in the winter and summer of 2012.

The cast of the Winter 2012 productions included Bridgette Hayes as Veronica, Rachel Kurnos as Vern, Bob Mussett as the Salesman for the Portsmouth, New Hampshire production, and James Bocock as the Salesman for the Cambridge, Massachusetts production.

The cast of the June 2012 production in Portsmouth included Mary Casiello as the Busker, Paul Strand as the Salesman, Elizabeth Locke as Veronica, Cassandra Heinrich as Vern, Teddi Kenick-Bailey as Nica, and Elise Williams as Andy.

❀

Special thanks to my undergraduate writing mentor David Crouse, and to my grad school mentors Michael Lowenthal, Christina Shea, Tony Eprile, and Rachel Kadish.

Thanks also to Crystal Lisbon and Mary Casiello for inviting me to coffee at Simon's that one day in 2011 to talk about collaborating on something. This book wouldn't exist if not for that meeting.

Mary, alongside Lissa Brennan and Chuck Galle, served as beta readers on the earliest prose version of this book.

Ali Russo and Viktor Herrmann served as my final beta readers.

Abbie Levesque copyedited. Any remaining errors are the result of my own stubbornness or stupidity. Abbie is the best.

ABOUT THE AUTHOR

E. Christopher Clark is the author of the Stains of Time series, a family saga with a hint of magical realism and a whole lot of time travel. His other books include the short story collections *Out of the Woods* and *Under the World*, the novella *The Seven Wives of Silver*, and a collection of poems cheekily titled *Bad Poetry Night*. His short stories have been published in *Live Free or Ride: Tales of the Concord Coach*, *River Muse: Tales of Lowell & the Merrimack Valley*, and the University of Hawaii's *Vice-Versa*. A graduate of Lesley University's MFA in Creative Writing program, he lives in Massachusetts with his wife and daughters.

echristopherclark.com

facebook.com/eccbooks

x.com/eccbooks

instagram.com/eccbooks

goodreads.com/eccbooks

pinterest.com/eccbooks

amazon.com/E.-Christopher-Clark/e/B00H0G94T0

www.ingramcontent.com/pod-product-compliance
Lightning Source LLC
Chambersburg PA
CBHW051307250626
47155CB00009B/3472